THE CURSE OF MCMILLAN CASTLE

CASTLE

BOOK 12.5 OF MORNA'S LEGACY SERIES

BETHANY CLAIRE

Cover Designed by Damonza

Available In eBook, Paperback, Hardback, & Large Print Paperback

eBook ISBN: 978-1-970110-23-4
Paperback ISBN: 978-1-970110-24-1
Hardback ISBN: 978-1-970110-25-8
Large Print Paperback ISBN: 978-1-970110-26-5

A curse, a ghost, and a painting that goes bump in the night might just be the key to their perfect romance.

Madeline knows firsthand that life rarely goes according to plan. If it did, her husband would still be alive, Scotland wouldn't be her home, and she wouldn't be living in the seventeenth century. Hardened by grief and broken dreams, Madeline hopes that a new life for her and her daughter might be enough to pull her from her years' long rut. Despite her best efforts in a new century, little changes. As the months pass, her wish for a happier tomorrow seems unlikely to come true. But when a newcomer with ties to the castle arrives in the village, Madeline's interest is piqued for the first time in years as she discovers maybe there's more reason to be hopeful than she originally thought.

Expert stone mason, Duncan, never dreamed that accepting a seemingly-harmless painting in exchange for his work would lead to such trouble. But after nights of no sleep make it clear that his new possession is indeed haunted, Duncan sets out to return the wretched piece of art back to its home at McMillan Castle. Determined only to rid himself of the art, Duncan's plans are derailed when he meets a lass so bonny he finds himself eager to accept work that will keep him at McMillan Castle longer than planned. As time passes and his feelings grow, Duncan discovers that perhaps his home is no longer the place he left behind.

Is their love strong enough for the two of them to overcome their baggage? Or will the story end with the curse that brought them together?

FREE BOOK - SUBSCRIBE TO MY NEWSLETTER

*T*oday when you sign up for my mailing list, I will send you a link where you can download *A Conall Christmas - A Novella* (Book 2.5 of Morna's Legacy Series) for FREE!

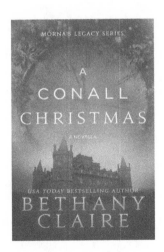

A Conall Christmas is not a Christmas tale as much as it is simply a love story. Adelle, Bri's mother, gets a second chance at love in this fun, uplifting book.

If you have already read it, I hope you will still choose to sign up for my mailing list just for the other benefits. I promise to never spam you. I will send out mailings only when I have news or special opportunities for you. And if you haven't read *A Conall Christmas* yet, you get it FREE today when you sign up.

When you sign up for my mailing list, you will be the first to know about new releases, upcoming events, and contests. You will also get sneak peeks into books and have opportunities to participate in special reader groups and occasionally get codes for free books.

Just click one of the links in the paragraphs above or go to http://eepurl.com/bqjLCT to sign up today. I can't wait to connect with you there.

PROLOGUE

any Years Earlier - McMillan Castle, 17ᵗʰ Century Scotland

*T*he clash of something heavy behind him caused Niall McMillan to spin towards the sound. For the third time this week, Osla's self-portrait had fallen from its place on the wall. It made no sense. He'd ensured it was properly secured only two days ago. And yet, once again, the portrait had nearly landed on his head. Had it fallen one second earlier, or had his steps been one step slower, it would have. Frowning, Niall bent and lifted the portrait until Osla's inky eyes were level with his own.

Not much scared Niall—he was the true monster to be feared within the castle—but as he stared into the inky eyes of his late sister-in-law, a shiver spread its way down his spine.

The portrait made him uneasy. It always had. From the moment Osla had finished the artwork, he'd objected to Baodan hanging it in the great hall. Not that the decision had been his to make. His brother was laird of McMillan Castle. At least for now.

He continued to stare into Osla's eyes as he willed the sense of unease inside him to go away. He hated looking at her. The likeness to her was unsettling, the way her eyes seemed to track him as he walked was almost supernatural. Not that he believed in any such nonsense. Flesh and blood, here and now, that was all there really was. Once dead, you were simply gone. Forever.

Still, ever since Osla's death, he wasn't the only one who found objection with the painting. On more than one occasion, he'd overheard servants whispering of how they didn't wish to be in the great hall alone. One of the cooks swore she'd seen the picture blink. And even their mother had told him in private that Osla's portrait looked as if it ached to breathe, and if she stared at it long enough, she wondered if perhaps she would truly see Osla's chest begin to rise and fall.

Breathe. Something Osla would never do again. Niall smiled as he thought back to the night the first part of his plan had been executed with such glorious perfection. The poison worked so much better than he'd ever imagined it would. And the weight she'd lost during her sickness made it easy for him to slide her out of the bedroom window once he'd wrapped the noose around the foolish woman's neck.

Thinking of Osla's death calmed him. The woman was dead. And with it, her secrets. This portrait could do him no harm now, even if it seemed determined to fly off its place on the wall with unsettling regularity.

Even so, perhaps it was better to rid all of them of its dreadful presence. Baodan didn't need the daily reminder of Osla's miserable face staring down at him. His brother was already gloomy enough since his wife's death. If Baodan asked where the portrait had gone, he would simply blame it on a servant—perhaps the one who'd dodged his advances the other day in the hallway outside his bedchamber. He didn't want that bitch around anymore either.

Two birds, one stone, as they say.

Smiling, his unease faded as he tucked the portrait beneath his arm and headed for the stables. He would go out for a long ride and give it to the first vagabond he happened upon once outside his brother's territory. Perhaps the wretch lucky enough to cross Niall's path could catch a price for the portrait, and the money received from it could see the poor man fed for at least a few moons.

It was a good thing he was doing, really. A generous thing. Sometimes it was good to do something entirely out of character.

CHAPTER 1

*M*acMillan Castle, 17*th* Century - Many Years Later -
October

Madeline

The sizzle of the stew bubbling out into the open fire it hung over caused me to jump as I stirred from my seat next to Henry's bed. Once again, he'd persuaded me to tell him stories about my old life—my life before my daughter Rosie and I abandoned life in the twenty-first century for a much more difficult, and much colder life, in the seventeenth century. Shivering— something I was quite certain I hadn't stopped doing since we arrived in this godforsaken century—I stood from my seat and reached for a heavy cloth so I could remove the old man's dinner from the fire.

A long-time servant of McMillan Castle, Henry knew all about the magic that had brought so many to this time and castle. After several years of confusion and questions, Baodan McMillan, laird of my new home, decided that it would be easier for everyone if all those who worked for the McMillans knew the truth of the magic and time travel that seemed to be the heartbeat of his home. Sworn to secrecy, and with the threat of magic over them if they ever did let the castle's secrets escape, no such slip-up had ever occurred.

The steam rising from the pot warmed me slightly as I stirred it to cool it down quickly enough for me to give some to Henry before I had to leave. Serving as a sort of home health nurse for Henry since his stroke was vastly different from the high-paced, non-stop work I'd been accustomed to at the Chicago hospital, but it had kept me busy enough for the past two months that I was now too tired when I crawled into bed at the end of the night to lie awake for hours and wonder if I'd ruined my daughter's life by uprooting her and bringing her here.

"Why doona ye go back, lass?"

I paused my stirring and looked through the steam toward the old man. "Why do you ask that?"

Deciding that the stew would have to just sit for a bit before serving, I walked over to the fire, poked at it a bit, and pulled Henry's sitting chair close to it before waving him over as he answered me.

"You're nae less miserable today than ye were when ye first came to help me two moons ago. Why did ye come here if ye enjoyed life in yer own time, so much?"

The damage from the stroke made Henry's words slow and difficult to understand, but after so many days with him, I'd learned how to decipher most of what he said to me.

It was easy for me to make life in my own time seem lovely when I regaled Henry with stories of running hot water and food delivery services, but the truth was, I'd been just as miserable there. Besides, we couldn't go back. There was nothing left for us in twenty-first century Scotland, and Chicago held too many terrible memories for us to ever have a home there, either.

"Do I behave miserably around you, Henry?"

He shook his head as he worked his way over toward me with

his cane. "Nae, but that doesna mean that ye are happy, lass. I can see how much it takes of ye to appear so."

I sighed. "Just because miserable is my normal, doesn't mean that everyone else should have to feel as I do when they're around me. Faking it is my only option. I used to think that one day the faking happy would stick, but I've since given up on that dream."

It was a horrible thing to admit, but it was true. Some part of my brain could vaguely remember a different version of me existing—a lighter, happier, less perpetually moody Madeline—but I was quite certain that girl had died along with Tim. The grief I'd once felt for him wasn't quite the same. I could now think of my late husband without my chest bearing down on me with such pain I thought I might die, but the person I'd been with him had yet to return, even all these years later.

The old man stared at me hard as I helped to lower him into his seat. "Pretending that much for that long will kill ye, Madeline."

"It hasn't yet." I smiled at him as I patted his hand in dismissal of the conversation before moving to return toward his dinner. The sun was already setting, and I couldn't stay with him as long today as I usually did.

"*Yet* is the word ye might should pay more mind to, lass."

With my back still toward him as I ladled his dinner into a wooden bowl, I responded. "I think you're overestimating my acting skills, Henry. I'm polite, but I don't think anyone would describe me as happy."

"Mayhap so. I doona wish to upset ye. Bring me my dinner, and tell me about something else that will make me envious that I wasna born in yer time."

Happy to move away from the current conversation, I reached for his spoon and smiled as I faced him. "I promise you I will tell you more stories tomorrow, but tonight I must leave a little early. Tomorrow is Rosie's birthday, and I have an important role to play in a surprise we have planned for her."

I still wasn't entirely sure what the surprise was. Cooper had been incredibly tight-lipped about it to me, but I left that part out of my explanation to Henry.

Henry smiled and nodded in understanding. He adored Rosie. At least twice a week she would come with me when I came to check in on him, and every time she came and I watched him interact with her, it saddened me that he didn't have any grandchildren of his own. The old man would've been so good with them.

"Ach, o'course ye must. How old is the wee lass?"

Just thinking of her being a teenager now made me ache inside. "She's not so wee anymore. She's thirteen today."

"Thirteen! Why, I married me Agatha when she was but thirteen."

I shuddered at the horrifying thought. "Rosie won't be getting married for another twenty years if I have anything to say about it."

Henry laughed and reached for his dinner. "Alas, 'tis unlikely that ye will have much to say about it after a few more years. Best enjoy this time with her while ye can."

Dread settled in my stomach as the truth I knew was spoken aloud. It seemed like yesterday I was bouncing her on my hip as she giggled and latched onto my hair before snuggling into my neck. I could still smell the sweet little baby smell of her if I closed my eyes and thought of it. How had time gone by so quickly?

At least the only young little gentleman currently determined to win over Rosie's heart was three years her junior. I still had quite some time before I had to worry about Rosie's heart being entirely broken.

CHAPTER 2

Cooper

Cooper stared down at his plans for Rosie's surprise as anxiety built inside him. There was too much to do and far too little time in which to do it. He needed this to happen for her tonight. Rosie needed one good thing that was just hers. He knew how she tried to hide it from him—Rosie was good at keeping her feelings hidden—but Cooper could see just how difficult the move here had been for her.

He jumped at the sound of a knock on his bedroom door, quickly sliding his carefully drawn plans out of sight just in case it was Rosie.

"Come in." He smiled as Rosie's mother slipped into the room and closed the door behind her. "Hello, Ms. Madeline."

She shook her head at him as she smiled. "Cooper, I've told you a hundred times. You don't have to call me 'Ms.' Just call me Madeline."

The young boy shrugged and shook his head. "Sorry, Ms.

Madeline. It just doesn't sound right without the Ms. at the beginning of it. What's up?"

Cooper watched as Madeline lowered herself to the ground and sat cross-legged beside him.

"What's up is that it's time for you to spill the beans. If I'm going to keep Rosie distracted for the next handful of hours, I need to know what the surprise is."

Cooper sighed and reached for the drawing underneath the edge of his bed.

"All right, I suppose it's time. But you promise you won't tell her, right?"

She held out her pinkie towards him. "Of course, I promise. I don't want to ruin the surprise for her."

Cooper took her pinkie as they swore secrecy then handed her the drawing.

"We are going to turn the old tower into a bedroom and study that's just for Rosie!"

The young boy's voice lifted with excitement as he smiled with pride at his idea. He did his best not to feel crestfallen when Madeline frowned at him.

"Oh, Cooper. There's no way I can let you do that. The tower was supposed to be your room. I heard E-o and your mother talking about it just a few weeks ago. You're getting older, and you've shared a room with your younger siblings for far too long. I know you've been looking forward to having your own space."

Relieved that worry over his own disappointment was Madeline's only reservation, Cooper smiled again and plunged ahead. "You're right. That was the plan, but I don't want that room. Truly, I don't. Besides, it only seems right to me that the oldest kid in the castle should have their own room, and now that's Rosie. She's a part of the McMillan clan now. She needs to feel like it. I know I need my own space too, but I get that all the time. Since I wake up so early, I usually have several hours a day where the entire castle is all mine. I'll be fine sharing with my siblings. Will you please just look at my plan and tell me if you think she will like it or not?"

Cooper extended the piece of paper toward her until she took it from him. He sat nervously as she stared down at his work until she smiled.

"What's this space here?"

Cooper leaned over to see her pointing at the bookcase his dad had been working on for the past two weeks.

"I'm calling it 'Rosie's Reading Corner.' I've had Harper busy gathering up a whole bunch of spooky books since I know that those are Rosie's favorite, and Dad went through just yesterday to pick them up. We're going to fill the bookcase with all sorts of things for Rosie to read, and Dad even built a cushioned seat that will sit up in the tower window so she can read in the sunshine or moonlight."

He said nothing, but Cooper frowned as Madeline reached over and tousled his curls. He knew people meant well, but he hated when people touched the top of his head. It made him feel like such a little child. He was in the double digits now—well on his way to adulthood.

"Coop, you truly are the sweetest boy that's ever lived. Rosie is going to love this. Are you going to be able to get it all done tonight?"

"Aye, we will."

Cooper and Madeline both turned toward the sound of E-o's voice in the doorway. Confidence filled Cooper at the sight of his stepdad. If E-o said there was time, Cooper had no doubt they would be able to get it done.

"Baodan, Grace, Mitsy, yer da and Kathleen, all are at the ready to help. All the furniture yer da has been working on is lined up and ready to be carried up from our secret location. As soon as

Madeline has Rosie tucked away for the evening, we are ready to begin."

Cooper jumped up from the floor and offered Madeline his hand. "Are you ready, Ms. Madeline? I'm so excited I can hardly stand it."

She smiled at him, and Cooper thought it was the happiest he'd ever seen Rosie's mom look.

"Yes, I'm ready. I'll make certain to keep her busy until you all are ready to show her."

Madeline took his hand, pulled herself up, then pulled him into a hug. "Thank you, Cooper. I can't wait to see Rosie's face."

He couldn't either. Her face was always his most favorite thing to look at. If she was truly happy about this, he couldn't even begin to imagine how completely radiant she would look then.

Cooper had never worked so hard in his entire life. Even with a handful of strong adults helping him, transforming E-o's old tower into a bedroom fit for Rosie was a tough job.

But now, with a few hours to spare, it was finished. Rosie would officially be able to wake up on her thirteenth birthday in her very own room.

It was the greatest accomplishment of his life.

He looked up in the direction of the hand that suddenly gave his shoulder a gentle squeeze. His father smiled down at him.

"You've done good, kid. I think this is just the thing Rosie needs to change her perspective about being here in this time. I know it's been an adjustment for her. This will surely help. It's perfect."

He smiled as he beamed up at his father with pride.

"It is, isn't it? It's the most perfect thing I've ever seen. Now, let's go get her so we can finally all go to bed. It's way past my bedtime."

Madeline

*F*or the first few hours, keeping Rosie distracted had been no problem. After gathering some dinner from the kitchen, spreading a blanket on the floor of our shared bedchamber, we'd been happy to have an indoor picnic, play some board games we'd brought with us from our own time, and visit. But as the evening hours crept past the time we usually went to bed, Rosie grew suspicious.

"What is going on, Mom? I do not understand why you're not letting me go to sleep. Usually you're insisting I do just that."

I scrambled for some sort of plausible answer. I really should've put more thought into how I would keep her away from the hustle and bustle going on outside of our room without ruining the surprise.

"There's something special supposed to happen with the moon tonight. I really wanted you to see it. Let's just stay up for a little while longer. One more game?"

She frowned at me and crossed her arms. God, she looked just like her father.

"How in the world do you know about seventeenth century astronomy stuff?"

"I..." I fumbled and knew I'd officially screwed up. "I don't. Umm...Baodan told me."

She shook her head and pushed herself up from the floor. "Nope. Baodan didn't tell you anything. What is going on? Why is there so much noise going on outside? I'm going to go..."

The door to our room flew open, interrupting her speech. Cooper stood in the doorway, grinning widely.

"It's ready. Come on, Rosie. We have a surprise for you."

As per usual, Rosie was suspicious of just about any scheme Cooper came up with. Despite the fact that she usually ended up enjoying whatever the young boy planned for them, Rosie seemed determined to resist the friendship.

She crossed her arms once again and furrowed her brows at him. "What sort of surprise? It's too late for surprises."

Cooper reached for her arm, pulling on it, until she uncrossed her arms as he began to tug her from the room. "It's not too late for this surprise. Come on. Come on."

I smiled as I followed them, laughing as Cooper determinedly dragged my daughter along behind him.

When we finally reached the staircase to the attic, Rosie stopped short. "I have absolutely no desire to see what is up there."

Cooper let loose of his grip on her arm and stepped up two steps before facing her so that they stood at eye level.

"Tough. You're going to see what's up there if I have to throw you over my shoulder and carry you up there myself."

I had to swallow hard to keep from laughing. Rosie was twice Cooper's size. There was no way he could carry her, but the seriousness of his tone was enough to keep Rosie from giving him any more hassle. Without another word, she followed him up to the tower room.

When I reached the doorway and looked inside, my eyes filled with tears, and although I couldn't see my daughter's face, I was almost certain hers were doing the same.

The room was perfect. Large and creepy—Rosie would adore it. And the thought put in to each and every space blew my mind.

"Is this…is this for me, Cooper?"

I stepped around her, needing to see her face. Looking at her wide eyes and flushed face made me start blubbering.

Cooper nodded and smiled. "Yes. You're going to be thirteen tomorrow. I thought you should wake up on your birthday in your very own room."

Silently, she threw her arms around him and hugged him tight —something I'd never seen her do before.

"Thank you, Cooper. This is the nicest thing anyone has ever done for me."

When she released him, Cooper's cheeks were as red as Rosie's hair.

"So, you like it?"

"I love it."

Cooper yawned, and his yawn quickly spread to everyone else in the room.

"Good. That's all I wanted. Now, let's go to bed. Happy Birthday, Rosie."

One by one we filed out of Rosie's new room. After everyone was gone, I lingered just past the doorway to watch her. Unaware that I could see her, Rosie smiled and began to spin around the room in delight.

I cried happy tears all the way back to what was now my own private room.

Perhaps moving here hadn't completely ruined my daughter's life. If I could find solace in nothing else, at least there was that.

CHAPTER 3

Duncan

For exactly three nights he'd been the reluctant owner of some strange woman's portrait, and for exactly three nights he'd woken in the middle of the night, drenched in sweat after the most horrid and repetitive dream. Duncan never dreamed, and yet ever since welcoming the portrait into his home, he couldn't seem to escape the onslaught of horrible visions that found him each night as he slept.

After lying sleeplessly for the latter half of the night, Duncan finally rose from his bed, moving to light a fire for warmth as he spoke to the stray village tabby cat that he allowed into his home each night so that she wouldn't freeze. He called her Tabitha. He wasn't sure if anyone else in the village had taken to her enough to give her a name. She ran wild during the daytime, but for some strange reason, after years of doing exactly as she pleased, Tabitha had fallen into the habit of coming to Duncan's home each evening, happy to seek the warmth of four walls and the comfort of someone's company during the night's darkest hours. Did that make Tabitha his? *No*, he thought to himself. He had no need of anything that required him, relied on him. He could barely take care of himself. Still, he couldn't deny that any night that Tabitha was a little late in her arrival, part of him began to worry dreadfully for her.

"What do ye say, Tabitha? Am I losing me mind, or is there something wrong with this here painting?" He pointed at the portrait for good measure as the fire he stoked began to roar. Tabitha—bless her—turned her head in the direction he pointed and meowed in appeasement.

He chuckled and nodded. "Aye, ye are right. Mayhap I am going mad. I'm speaking to ye as if I expect ye to answer me back. Though the lad did seem in quite a hurry to be rid of this here lady, dinna he?"

It was no wonder that he'd made less from his work this year than any year prior. How did he expect to make what he needed to, when he accepted gifts rather than currency for work?

He continued speaking to Tabitha, even as the cat turned away from him, no longer interested in the conversation.

"Either way, whether it be the painting or me own mind, I doona think I can keep her in the house another night."

The fire crackled beside him, and for a moment he had the mind to walk across the room, pick up the portrait and throw it into the flames, but as he stared into the eyes of the woman within, something stopped him.

Duncan wasn't a believer in the supernatural. Unlike many in Scotland, he didn't fear that he might one day wander into the land of the faeries, and he didn't feel the need to stay indoors during a full moon. But if anything could change his mind, it would be the portrait that hung just a few paces from him. It filled his entire room with a sense of unease he didn't care for.

"What do ye say, Tabitha? Do ye wish to follow me to me mother's house? Ye ken she is likely to have fresh milk that she will spoil ye with."

His mother was the village oddity. Happily widowed for decades, if not for the protection their laird provided her, Duncan was certain she would've been burned as a witch years ago. She wasn't a witch, at least not that Duncan knew of. But she did have an unusual proclivity for all things occult. Perhaps she could give him some idea of what to do with the dreadful painting and how to find some restful sleep once again.

Dressing quickly, Duncan reached for the portrait before opening the door to the cold October air. As expected, Tabitha shot out of his home with such speed that he knew there was no chance of her following him over to his mother's like some docile, obedient dog. It would be evening before he saw the wee beastie again.

It was just as well. He understood Tabitha's wildness, and he had no desire to change it. No one had ever been able to tame him, either.

It was early still. Although most of the village still slept, he knew his mother would be awake, most likely sewing by her fire.

He knocked gently on her door before opening it as he called out to her. "Do ye ever sleep past the rising of the sun?"

His mother twisted in her chair and frowned at him. "Why ever would I do that, lad? At my age, I doona have time to waste sleeping. I doona wish to miss a moment of whatever time I have left snoring it away."

He smiled at her and pulled up another chair near the fire before returning back to the front door of her home to pick up the portrait he'd set just inside upon entering.

"Some would say that sleep might see ye live longer."

"Some say a fair manner of nonsense, Duncan. Ye most of all.

Now, why are ye here so early? Ye have never had any trouble sleeping past the rising of the sun, as ye say, and what did ye bring in here with ye?"

Carrying the portrait over to her, he sat down across from his mother and set the bottom edge of the portrait's frame on the floor so that his mother could see it.

"I think this lassie may be haunting me."

"Haunting ye? Ye doona believe in ghosts."

"I doona. But each night since she came into me possession, I have had the most terrible dreams of the woman portrayed in the painting."

"Ye never dream."

"Aye. I ken."

His mother sighed and leaned back in her chair. "Just how did ye come into possession of this portrait? And what precisely, are ye dreaming?"

"Old man Travis gave it to me in exchange for some stonework I did for him. He dinna tell me until the job was done that he dinna have the means to pay me. And I dinna notice at the time just how eager he seemed to be rid of this lassie. And as for the dreams, 'tis the same dream each night. I dream that I am sleeping, but the sound of something rattling startles me awake. I wake to the fire in me home raging and this here portrait rattling furiously against the wall. When I rise from the bed and approach her, I can see tears streaming down her face. When I reach for her, her mouth opens and the wretched lass screams violently at me. Then I awake covered in sweat despite the chill in the air all around me."

The expression on his mother's face was stern. Pushing her feet into the ground, Duncan watched as she scooted a little further away from him.

"And ye thought it a grand idea to bring this item into me home then, did ye?"

Duncan chuckled. "I willna leave her here with ye. I wish to ken if ye have any suggestions for what I might do with her. I must have a peaceful night's sleep, or I fear I truly shall go mad."

"Lift it in front of me so that I might look at her more closely."

Standing, Duncan did as instructed and held the picture high enough so that the strange woman's eyes were level with his mother's.

He watched as she stared at it for a long while. Eventually, after studying it, she reached out and brushed her finger across the signature at the bottom, before pulling back to look at her own finger.

"Ye may set it down now, lad. The portrait is signed in someone's blood. I would wager her own. If the woman in the painting is dead, her soul may be trapped within it. Best ye return her home and find out. She is unlikely to find any peace here."

Duncan swallowed hard as he lowered the portrait to the floor.

"Ye canna be in earnest, aye? Such a thing couldna trap a soul."

She nodded firmly. "Aye. It can, and I believe it has. Ye should wrap her up and leave at once."

"And where precisely am I to go with her? How do ye ken where her home is?"

His mother pointed to the bloody signature. "Osla McMillan. Ye must go to McMillan territory."

McMillan territory was at least a four day's ride from their own. With weather as cold as it was now, it might take him even longer.

Before he could utter a word, his mother spoke up again. "Doona worry, son. I shall let Tabitha into yer house each night and let her out each morning. Ye do ken that ye are the owner of a cat now, aye?"

He shook his head as he stood and reached for the portrait. "I ken no such thing."

His mother laughed as he walked toward the door once again.

"It doesna truly matter whether ye ken it or no'. 'Tis true enough. Safe travels, son. See this lassie safely home. Help her find some peace. Then ye shall sleep soundly again, I'm certain."

CHAPTER 4

Rosie

*A*ll of the candles in Rosie's room were burned down to stubs, and her vision blurred after hours of reading through the night. Goosebumps covered both her arms as she breathlessly turned one page after the other. Never in her life had she read such a scary story. Never in her life had she enjoyed a book so much.

Maybe, just maybe, life in the seventeenth century wouldn't be so horrible after all. At least there was now somewhere for her to escape to when everything just seemed like too much. So many things had seemed like too much lately. The move to this time, her mother's never-ending unhappiness, the lack of privacy everywhere within the castle, the horrifying discovery that she was starting to grow boobs. The whole year had just been rough.

Yawning, Rosie finally closed the nearly-finished book and pushed herself out of the window seat where she'd spent the whole night reading. She'd not slept a wink, and no one had known the difference. Her new room was officially her favorite place in all the world.

Turning back toward the window, Rosie looked out into the night sky to try and gauge the time. Still dark to be sure, but nearly morning. Cooper would be awake.

Truth was, she didn't mind the kid. But there was no way she could let him know that. He was already in love with her. Rosie feared that if Cooper knew that she really did consider him a friend, his affection for her would become unbearable. She couldn't have that.

Today, however, Rosie knew she should make an exception. After what Cooper had done for her with this room, the boy deserved a little bit of kindness.

And after a long, sleepless night of reading, Rosie was starving. She knew there was a cake for her somewhere in the castle kitchen. Perhaps, Cooper would be up for a little bit of mischief.

Smiling, Rosie dressed and looked herself over in the mirror.

Thirteen. Was there possibly a more complicated age? Surely not. No longer a child, but certainly not a woman. It was the most stuck-in-the-middle age ever. If it were up to her, she would just skip all the way to eighteen and be done with it.

Tucking her red curls behind her ears, Rosie brushed the sleep from her eyes and quietly made her way out of her bedroom tower.

She'd never been up and about in the castle when it was so quiet. It brought to mind the ghost story she'd just been reading, and despite her love of all things spooky, her feet moved a little more quickly than was absolutely necessary as she ran through the castle hallways in her search for Cooper. When she reached the dining hall and saw a candle burning, she knew she'd found him.

"Cooper." She whispered his name, and gently knocked on the wall so he would turn toward her.

"Rosie?"

Rosie could see Cooper twist toward her, but realizing that he probably couldn't see her in the darkness, she hurried toward the candlelight.

"Yeah, it's me. You hungry?"

Cooper smiled and popped up from his place on the floor. "It's weird. I'm always hungry nowadays. Maybe it means I'm finally growing."

Rosie snorted. "I wouldn't count on it. I bet you're always going to be that small."

Cooper didn't take her bait. Much to her disappointment, he never did.

"Wrong. I'm definitely not going to stay this small. You just wait and see."

"I'm not holding my breath."

Again, Cooper didn't bite and instead changed the subject. "What are you doing up so early, anyway? Please tell me you didn't sleep badly. I wanted you to have the best night's sleep ever."

She smiled even more widely. "I didn't sleep at all, Cooper! It was the best night ever."

"Huh?"

"I read all night long, one of the stories you got for me. Thank you, Cooper. Really."

Rosie didn't miss how Cooper's shoulders relaxed a little bit once he knew she was pleased.

"Well, that does sound like a pretty good night. I've never been able to stay up the whole night reading, but I bet someday I'm able to get there. Now, what are we going to eat?"

Rosie shrugged, guiltily. "Birthday cake, maybe?"

Cooper bent to lift his candle from its place on the floor and held the flame up between them. His expression was hesitant.

"You want to cut into it before the celebration tonight?"

Rosie nodded.

"Won't we get into trouble?"

Rosie was thirteen now. Weren't thirteen years olds supposed to get into a little bit of trouble? And Cooper was way past due for some. She shrugged again. "So? Sometimes, trouble is fun. Besides, it's *my* birthday cake. Shouldn't I be able to eat it whenever I want?"

Cooper furrowed his brows and lifted his shoulders reluctantly. "I don't know. I don't feel great about it."

"I bet you'll feel better about it when we're elbow deep in some chocolate cake. You're in, right?"

Cooper sighed and gave her a nod. "Don't you know by now, Rosie? I'd follow you anywhere. Now, let's go enjoy this cake because I have a feeling it might be all we are allowed to eat for the next three days after we're caught."

Rosie wrinkled her nose at him in confusion. "You think they're going to starve us as punishment? Boy, you really haven't been in very much trouble before, have you?"

"Nope."

Rosie reached for his free hand and began to pull him toward the kitchen. "Well, then it's time for you to figure out just how not-scary trouble really is. Trust me, it will be fine."

While she wasn't entirely sure that her reassurances to Cooper were true, she was too far in to back out now.

CHAPTER 5

Madeline

*R*osie's birthday played out differently than my daughter had imagined it would. When the cook happened upon Rosie and Cooper cowering in the corner of the kitchen, their faces covered in icing, and alerted me to what had happened, I made the executive decision to let the day pass without a word about it. I knew my daughter. Part of her wanted to get in trouble. She possessed the same rebellious streak in her that I'd had myself at her age. Each little harmless act of rebellion she committed now was like a giant red flashing warning sign of the hell that awaited me in the years to come.

It was for that reason that I chose to ignore the birthday cake fiasco. There would be battles in the years ahead that would be worth fighting with her— sneaking birthday cake wasn't one of them.

Instead, without saying a word to Rosie, I instructed the cook to leave the cake out in the dining hall so that everyone in the castle could help themselves to it throughout the day. When it was time for dinner, we made no presentation of the cake, sang her no birthday song, and blew out no candles. We still ate Rosie's favorite meal, gifted her presents, and behaved pleasantly as if nothing had happened. The only difference was that the evening progressed as if there had never been a cake made solely for her.

She got the point really quickly.

By the next morning, she had apologized to me, and the cook, twice, and poor Cooper had done so at least a half dozen times.

In the week that followed Rosie's birthday, I saw little of her. She spent every spare moment in her new bedroom. Most days she was still asleep when I left to make my home check-ins with the handful of villagers I'd now added to my little 'stay-busy-so-you-don't-cry-yourself-to-sleep' home care practice.

Eventually though, I began to miss the time that I'd grown accustomed to each day with my daughter when we were sharing a room. So one morning I decided I simply couldn't do without a few hours with my ginger-headed teenager.

When my knock on her bedroom door was met without answer, I slowly cracked it open to see her sleeping with her arms high above her head, a book spread open on her chest. If I were to wager on it, I'd bet she'd only been asleep for a couple of hours at best.

Smiling, I walked over, picked up the book, and marked its place before bending down to kiss her on the forehead.

"Wake up, sleepyhead. Will you come with me to Henry's this morning? He's been wanting to give you your birthday gift for a while now."

Rosie groaned and stretched before slowly fluttering her eyes open. "He has a gift for me?"

Of course that had gotten her attention.

"Yes. Can you get dressed quickly? It looks like it's going to rain soon. I'd like to get there before the sky opens up."

She nodded sleepily, and sat up in the bed. "Give me five. I'll meet you downstairs."

———

Duncan

*A*fter days of keeping the portrait safe during his travels to McMillan territory, Duncan wasn't about to allow the sudden rainstorm to destroy the painting now that he was within sight of McMillan Castle. Upon arriving at his destination, however, he was entirely unsure how to proceed.

While it stood to reason that if the lassie's last name was McMillan, the portrait most likely belonged at McMillan Castle itself, he didn't know whether it was wise to ride straight up to the castle. He knew nothing of the McMillans. More than a few lairds he knew of wouldn't take kindly to a stranger arriving on the castle steps unannounced and requesting entry. Mayhap it was wisest to knock on the door of one of the villagers and inquire into the temperament of the territory's laird.

Blinking through the rain, Duncan closely observed the village as he looked for a dry place to seek refuge from the rain.

"If I can find ye a stable for a while, will ye enjoy a nice rest?"

In Tabitha's stead, Duncan found that he'd taken to speaking to his horse much like he'd done to the strange wild beastie that visited him at home each night.

The horse said nothing but pulled in the direction of the stables in the distance.

"There ye go, lad. Ye wish to be out of this weather just as much as I do."

With the stable empty, and the cottage next to it quiet in response to his knocking, Duncan secured his horse within the stables and left payment outside the door of the empty home before leaving in search of another home that might be amiable to his questions.

Not far from the stables, he could see a cottage alight with candles and could make out the figures of at least three people within. It would do well enough.

It took only a moment for the door to swing open.

The smile disappeared from the face of the lass before him as she looked him over. Without a word, she turned back to address someone else inside the home.

"Henry, were you expecting anyone today? Do you know this man?"

By God, the lass spoke strangely. She wasn't from Scotland, to be sure, but where then? He'd never heard such plain speech in his life.

"Nae, lass. I'm expecting no one, but let him in all the same. He is drenched from head to toe."

Duncan watched as the strange woman stepped aside to permit him entry. He nodded in thanks as he stepped inside and spoke for the first time.

"My apologies for the intrusion. Ye doona ken me, sir. I am no' from these parts. I merely wish to ask ye a question or two then I shall continue on my way."

The lass next to him spoke up again. "Henry doesn't have any money to give you, sir. If you are a beggar, you will have to look elsewhere."

The road must've been harsher to him than he realized if he looked rough enough to be mistaken for a beggar.

"Nae, lass. I am no' a beggar. I have urgent business with Laird McMillan. I only mean to inquire as to his nature. The laird doesna ken I am coming, and I doona wish to be met with hostility."

For the first time, the young woman seated next to the old man smiled in his direction and spoke up. "You mean, Baodan? No

32

worries there. Mom greeted you with way more hostility than anyone at the castle will. You've already met McMillan Castle's scariest resident."

The young girl laughed, and Duncan watched as her mother crossed her arms and frowned at the girl before returning her gaze to him. The young lassie's speech was just as unfamiliar to him as her mother's.

"I apologize. I should not have assumed. It's just that Henry is too kind, and I wouldn't want anyone to take advantage of him. What exactly is the nature of your business with Baodan?"

Despite the woman's apology, her tone said everything that her words did not—she remained suspicious of him.

"I believe I am in possession of something that belongs to him. I wish to return it. Then I shall be on me way back home."

The woman said nothing as she looked him over once more, assessing him, judging him. The intensity of her gaze made him nervous, and he thought that perhaps the wee lass had been right about her being the castle's scariest resident, for there had been no one in a fair number of years who set him quite as on edge as she.

"Fine. You can follow us back up to the castle once the rain stops. Take off those wet boots and you can join us by the fire."

CHAPTER 6

Madeline

*W*hy in the world was I being so mean to this probably-harmless stranger? I tried to determine the answer as I watched him interact with Henry and my daughter as we all sat around the fire waiting for the storm to pass.

The man was kind, witty, and intelligent, but each and every time he directed any statement or question toward me, I responded with the friendliness of a thorn bush. What was the matter with me?

The question tormented me as the afternoon passed, and the rain continued. It was only when the distant part of my mind that was vaguely paying attention to the conversation in the room picked up on Rosie's mention of her late father that it hit me immediately.

I was attracted to this man. Instantly. Immediately. And my body and mind's reaction to the foreign chemical reaction was to throw up my strongest defense mechanism—to behave like a super, cranky bitch.

It was the first time in fifteen years I'd had such a visceral reaction to anyone. And it was the first time since Tim had died that some part of the person I'd been before had attempted to flicker back to life.

But rather than allow some part of my humanity to return, the most broken parts of me had rebelled against it.

It was only further proof of just how hopeless any chance of my life ever being normal again really was.

Claustrophobic and frustrated with myself, I stood and looked out the window toward the castle before interrupting the conversation of the others in the room.

"It's just sprinkling now, and it's getting dark. We'd better head to the castle."

"Aye."

The stranger—I still didn't know his name, although I was certain he'd said it—stood, thanked Henry for his hospitality and made his way to the door.

"Allow me to fetch me horse. 'Twill only take me a moment."

Once he was far enough away that he could no longer hear her, Rosie walked over to me and grabbed my hand.

"Are you okay, Mom? You've been acting strange all afternoon."

"Of course, I am. Just frustrated that the whole day got away from me due to this weather."

Rosie narrowed her eyes at me. She wasn't buying it, but rather than pry, she pretended that she did.

"Okay. Surely Baodan will invite Duncan to stay for dinner, right? He should really allow him to stay the night at the castle, too. I hate the thought of him having to be back out on the road again in this weather."

Duncan. I made a mental note so that I would remember his name.

"I'm sure no one will mind him staying for dinner, but he

should seek shelter at the inn if he doesn't wish to be on the road. The castle is full up, as it is."

Rosie frowned at me, but said nothing as we watched Duncan approach.

"Thank ye both for yer kindness in allowing me to walk with ye to the castle."

I gave him a curt nod and pointed to his horse.

"Just keep your horse behind us. I don't want to step in its excrement."

Rosie turned horrified eyes on me as we stepped away from Henry's house to begin the short walk to the castle.

What the hell was wrong with me? I seriously needed to get a grip.

In complete contrast to the way I'd treated Duncan and completely in line with Rosie's predictions, the first person we ran into at McMillan Castle after seeing Duncan's horse to the castle stables—my stepmother, Kenna—greeted Duncan with nothing but warmth.

"Who do the two of ye have with ye? Have ye picked up a new friend?"

Duncan spoke up beside me before either Rosie or myself could answer her. "They were kind enough to allow me to walk with them after the rain. Me name is Duncan. Might ye be the mistress of this castle?"

Kenna blushed and waved a dismissive hand. "Nae, lad. No' anymore. I am the laird's mother. Might I be of assistance to ye?"

Duncan nodded. "Aye, mayhap so. I recently came into possession of something I believe belongs here. I have come to return it."

Kenna cocked her head to the side in confusion before gripping his arm and pulling him further into the castle entry hall.

"Something that belongs here, ye say? How then did it end up in yer possession?"

"I am a stone mason, me lady. Recently, I undertook some work for a man back home. When I was finished, he couldna pay. Instead, he offered what I have returned to ye today. I doona ken how this item found its way to the man who gave it to me."

"And why precisely would ye return something that was gifted to ye? And how do ye ken it originates from here?"

Before continuing, Duncan glanced cautiously over at my daughter. "Forgive me, but I doona ken if 'tis best for me to say in front of the child. I doona wish to scare her."

Rosie wasted no time in speaking up for herself. "First, I'm not a child. Second, you're worried about scaring me? Don't be. I love being scared. Please don't stop on my account."

I nodded as Duncan's eyes searched mine for permission. Rosie and I were both too intrigued to leave Duncan alone with Kenna without hearing the whole story.

"It's fine. Go ahead."

Duncan frowned, but said nothing as he returned his attention to Kenna. "Verra well then. Me lady, I carry with me a portrait of a lass I believe must be related to ye. This lassie's soul has tormented me each night I've had this here painting in me possession. 'Tis me hope that returned to her home, she shall return to peace once more, and I might finally have a good night's sleep."

I watched as Kenna's face paled even before Duncan moved to undrape the portrait. The moment the portrait was revealed to her, I saw her eyes begin to roll, and I rushed to catch her as she fell.

CHAPTER 7

Duncan

*L*ady Kenna had seen the portrait before—the way her face paled before she collapsed backwards into Madeline's arms made that clear. He moved quickly after watching the Lady Kenna swoon, laying the portrait down on its back before hurrying to offer his assistance.

The woman regained consciousness quickly. Her eyes fluttered open almost as quickly as they'd rolled back into her head.

"Ach, me apologies. I dinna mean to upset ye so."

Madeline placed one hand on Kenna's cheek before looking up at him. "Help me get her into the sitting room. Her skin is so cold. Let's get her seated by the fire."

With a quick nod, Duncan lowered himself and scooped Kenna into his arms. The woman was petite and lighter than most children.

The old woman protested immediately. "I am fine, truly. Ye can set me down. Ye only took me by surprise is all."

Relieved that she'd found her voice and that the color was quickly returning to her face, Duncan smiled down at her, but he made no move to set her back down on two feet.

"I'll see ye to a chair, just as I was asked."

"Then do so quickly, and go and gather the portrait straight away. I doona wish for Baodan to see it."

It was no more than a few long strides to the chair Madeline directed him toward. The moment he lowered Kenna into the seat, he turned to gather the portrait but found that Rosie was already carrying it into the sitting room.

He nodded at her as he reached for the wide frame. "Thank ye, lass."

He could see in the young lassie's eyes that she worried for Kenna, for the moment he relieved her of the portrait, the young girl rushed to kneel down by Kenna's side.

"Are you really okay? Are you sure I shouldn't go and get Baodan?"

Duncan watched as Kenna's hand shot out and gripped at Rosie's arms.

"Aye, lass. I'm fine. And doona ye dare go and get Baodan. He is the last person I wish to be in this room. Will ye go and close the door so that the four of us might have some privacy?"

Duncan stepped out of Rosie's path as she hurried to close the door to the sitting room. Kenna said nothing else until the door was securely closed.

"None of ye are to tell anyone else about this painting, do ye understand?"

Duncan said nothing—there was no one for him to tell. He knew no one else in McMillan Castle outside of those in the very room he found himself in now.

All he wanted to do was leave. He'd returned the portrait. His part was done.

"If ye will excuse me, I think it best if I bid ye farewell. If ye truly are fine, I doona wish to intrude on ye any longer. I only wanted to return what belonged to ye."

Kenna shot him a look that stopped him in his tracks.

"Ye, sir, are no' leaving the castle, this night. 'Tis too late now. But we canna tell anyone else why ye are really here, which is precisely why I had wee Rosie shut the door to this room. Sit. We must fabricate a story."

What had he gotten himself into? He should've just burned the painting when the impulse first struck him and been done with it.

Madeline

While my stepmother might've been fine after her brief fainting spell, I couldn't say the same for myself. My hands shook uncontrollably as I stood near the fire, watching Kenna forbid Duncan to leave. Kenna was tough. She was feisty. Seeing her so rattled nearly scared me to death.

For the first time since directing Duncan to help me move her, I spoke, and my voice shook with every word. "Kenna, what the hell is going on? Who is that in the painting?"

Before Kenna could answer me, Duncan's arm came around my back to steady me.

"I think ye should sit as well, lass. Ye doona look well."

I didn't feel well. Nodding, I allowed him to usher me over to a chair opposite Kenna.

When I was seated, Kenna answered me.

"Take a deep breath, lass. We doona need ye dropping to the floor, too. I dinna mean to frighten ye. 'Twas shock is all."

I did as she bid, and the intake of air seemed to steady my voice just a little.

"You didn't answer my question, Kenna. Who is that?"

"'Tis Osla. Baodan's first wife."

"What?" My voice broke like a hormonal teenage boy. "His first wife? How did I not know about that?"

The truth was, I imagined there was a lot about the McMillans I didn't know. My father could speak for hours if asked about something, but he had never really been one to volunteer information, and I'd never really asked him or Kenna much about McMillan history. Still, the thought of Baodan being with anyone else besides Mitsy was difficult for me to comprehend.

I watched Kenna carefully, and the heaviness that fell over her features saddened me all the way through to my core.

When she spoke again, her voice was low and quiet. "We doona speak of her much, though mayhap we should. Osla was a fine lass, kind and gentle. She dinna deserve what happened to her. It took Baodan too long to forgive himself for all that happened during those dreadful years."

"What happened?" Rosie's voice, also quiet, spoke up next to Kenna, her hand slowly giving her grandmother's hand a gentle squeeze of comfort.

"She died. For a verra long time, we thought the lass had taken her own life. In truth, she was another one of Niall's victims."

While this was the first I'd heard of Baodan's first wife, I had heard stories of Kenna's second son. Kenna, understandably, rarely spoke of him. I couldn't begin to imagine how difficult it must be for a mother to reconcile that one's son was capable of murder. The grief, the anger, the confusion and guilt, and the fact that Kenna had moved on from all of it as bravely as she had was a testament to her strength.

When none of us said anything, Kenna continued. "I remember the day I noticed her portrait was missing. I thought mayhap the sight of her each day had been too difficult for Baodan to bear, so he'd removed it himself. I never asked him about it for that verra

42

reason. I suspect he wondered the same of me. Regardless, I do ken that seeing this now would upset him." Kenna paused and glanced in Duncan's direction. "I agree with ye that the lass should be here, but I doona wish for Baodan to see it. Whatever presence ye may have sensed within this painting, I've no doubt the disturbance to ye shall end now that ye've seen her home. I shall see her portrait tucked away in the cellar for safekeeping. In the meantime, we must think of another reason to explain yer arrival here."

Kenna stopped and stared at Duncan as if she expected him to come up with some sort of believable excuse. As I watched him, my earlier feelings shifted. Rather than a desire to greet him with snark, I wanted to help him.

How confused he must be—sitting there silently, wanting to leave—while Kenna went on about people he knew nothing about. He'd done a kindness by returning the painting, and now he was being asked to lie to the laird of McMillan Castle.

I turned to look at him as I tried to offer him a lifeline. "You did say you were a stone mason, didn't you? I've noticed that part of the east wall surrounding the castle has crumbled in a pretty large section. Maybe Kenna heard word of your good work from someone in the village and sent a messenger asking you to come here?"

Duncan looked at me hesitantly, then nodded before glancing over at Kenna for approval.

"Aye, mayhap so. I noticed the wall meself as we approached. 'Tis a large job, but I would be more than happy to take it on, though 'twill take me the better part of a moon to do so. Do ye think it possible for me to procure lodging somewhere near the castle for that long?"

Kenna smiled and rose from her seat, seemingly no worse for wear from her fainting spell.

"Aye, o'course. The inn in the village is run by the two kindest people ye shall ever meet. We will pay for yer lodgings and will o'course pay for the work that ye do here. 'Tis a bonny plan. Madeline, do ye mind seeing Duncan to the dining hall and making introductions? I shall tend to this painting and be along for dinner shortly."

CHAPTER 8

Duncan

*N*ever before had he found himself in the presence of such strange people. So many of them spoke with the same strange accent. He couldn't place it. It was plain. Simple. Unrefined. And while they all spoke English, he was unaware of any English-speaking country in or out of Scotland that spoke in such a way.

It wasn't only the sound of their speech that surprised him. The words that came out of the lassie's mouths came as a shock. They all spoke so openly. It was clear that among this lot, there was no real rank or order among them. All were free to say what they wished. Duncan found it remarkably refreshing.

Even the children sat at the table with the rest of them, and the one seated directly next to him was especially vocal.

"Go on. Give it a taste. I know it doesn't look appetizing, but I promise it's good. Our cook here is excellent."

Duncan looked down at the young lad and smiled as he tried to make his best guess as to the child's age. He almost certainly looked younger than he actually was.

"Aye. 'Tis true. I've already tasted it. 'Tis only I've found myself distracted by the conversation around the table. What is yer name, lad?"

He turned back toward his dinner as the boy answered him.

"I'm Cooper. I'm Grace's and E-o's, and Jeffrey's and Kathleen's son."

Duncan couldn't help the way his eyebrows lifted at the boy's words. What sort of a place did he find himself in? He'd heard stories of such living arrangements in other countries, but certainly not in Scotland.

"Oh?" The question slipped out before he could catch himself.

Cooper laughed beside him. "It's a long story. I forget that our little life is strange to most people here."

Duncan hurried to try and find some way to redirect the conversation. "'Tis none of my business, lad. Have ye…"

The boy interrupted him before he could continue. "Nah. It's okay. It'll be less weird to you once I explain it. Jeffrey isn't my real dad, you see. I never knew my real dad. He was gone before I was born. But Jeffrey and my mom, Grace, were real good friends, and he stepped in as my dad my whole life, so he's really my dad in every way that matters. But later, when I was a little older, Mom fell in love with E-o, and Dad fell in love with Kathleen, so now I have another bonus Mom and Dad. You see?"

Duncan's shoulders relaxed as he listened to the boy's explanation. "Ah. I do see. Ye are a lucky lad then. One canna ever have too much family, aye?"

Cooper nodded. "Exactly."

Madeline

I ate little over dinner. I was too busy listening to Duncan interact with Cooper. It had taken everything in me not to burst into laughter as I watched the look of shock and horror cross Duncan's face as Cooper told him just who all he belonged to. While common in my own time, nothing of the sort was common here. But Duncan's restrained and understanding response only served to increase my opinion of him further.

He was just as lovely with everyone else at the table. But while he engaged with all of them with just as much kindness as he had Henry earlier in the day, he seemed much less at ease with the McMillans than he had with my elderly patient.

It made perfect sense. We were an odd lot, and we all knew it. While I had exactly zero experience with the workings and livings of other Scottish castles, I knew that most of them didn't run in the way ours did.

If Duncan did have such experience with other castle households, I imagined this dinner had to be an overwhelming juxtaposition. All of us women spoke freely and loudly, Baodan didn't rule over us in any real way, and we interacted with those who served us as if they were real humans and not just silent animate objects moving in and out of the room.

I couldn't tell as I watched him whether or not he found the oddity of us appealing or completely unnerving. Perhaps it was a little of both.

The dinner was nearly over when Duncan spoke to me for the first time since sitting down.

"Are ye well, lass? Ye havena said a word since we sat down. Mayhap I smell, aye? 'Tis likely I do. Me apologies."

I turned toward him and smiled as I shook my head. He did

smell, but not badly. He had a manly, musky scent that I honestly quite enjoyed.

"I'm perfectly well. And you don't smell. I've just been listening, trying to decipher what you're thinking about all of us."

His expression was guarded as he narrowed his eyes. "The truth?"

I nodded. "Always."

"The entire lot of ye are the bonniest clan I've ever spent time with, and I canna tell if that means I should sneak away in the night and ne'er come back here for something is afoot, or if I should rent some land from yer Laird and build up a home and ne'er leave."

I liked the thought of him never leaving, even as stupid as the thought felt inside my mind. I didn't know this man, but my judgment of him was as agreeable as his was of us. He was one of the bonniest men I'd ever met, as well.

"Which way are you leaning?"

He smiled again, and I smiled as I looked at the way the corners of his eyes crinkled when he did so.

"I doona ken yet. 'Twill take me a few more days among ye to decide."

I chuckled. "Fair enough."

"Might I ask ye a question, Madeline?"

Butterflies took flight inside my stomach at the sound of my name rolling off his tongue. Jesus, I was in trouble.

"You can."

"Where are all of ye from? Many of ye are no' from Scotland, and I ken well enough that most of ye are no' related, so how did so many of ye end up here? And where precisely do ye hail from? I've ne'er heard such speech before."

Shit, I thought to myself as I scrambled to come up with an explanation. Duncan wasn't a permanent resident of McMillan territory. He wasn't allowed to know the truth about any of us.

"Um...you see...you're right, we're not Scottish. Most of us are from outside of London."

"London?" He frowned as he crossed his arms in disbelief.

"None of ye sound as if ye are from London, lass."

"We've traveled a lot. Over time, a bunch of accents have just blended together, I guess."

"I've traveled much, too. Me journeys havena caused me to lose the Scottish lilt in me voice."

I shrugged, drowning in my effort to come up with some sort of believable lie.

When I glanced over to see Kenna pushing herself away from the table as she waved at Duncan, I practically knocked over my chair in my effort to get away from the table.

"Oh, look! I think Kenna is ready for you two to visit with Baodan about your new job. I'll get out of the way so you three can talk."

I could feel his frown boring into my back as I all but ran away from him.

CHAPTER 9

Duncan

"Ye needn't escort me to the inn, lass. I am certain I could find me way there well enough."

The poor lass looked dead on her feet. It was no wonder. Secrets added weight to one's soul, and now they were both the bearers of a secret whether they wished to be or not.

He didn't like lying to the laird, but he could see Kenna's genuine desire to protect him—even if he didn't understand all of the specifics of which she'd spoken.

And it wasn't only their shared secret that must weigh on Madeline's shoulders. The lass had more secrets, he was sure of it. She was not from London. None of them were. But why lie to him about it? Why would she not wish for him to know about her homeland?

"I'm sure you could find it, but I want to speak to Isobel and let her know that Kenna is going to see them taken care of, and explain that you might be staying with them for a while."

Thinking of his newfound work pleased him. He could trust a

laird to pay currency he could use. The income would be a welcome relief after far too many scarce months of work.

"Aye, fine, but someone else must come along. 'Twouldn't be proper for the two of us to be out at night all alone."

Madeline groaned and rolled her eyes as they stopped short in front of the grand entryway door.

"I promise you, it's fine. No one in this territory will think anything of it."

Duncan regarded her hesitantly but chose not to argue the point further as she plunged ahead of him into the darkness.

"Madeline, is there a messenger that ye trust? One I could use to send a letter back home?"

"Yes, of course. Bring the letter with you to the castle tomorrow, and I'll make sure it gets to the man Baodan uses most. Do you have a wife and children back home you need to let know you'll be away for longer than planned?"

"Nae. I've nae children nor wife. 'Tis me mother. She has promised to care for a stray cat that loves to call me home hers when the sun sets. I just wish to tell her how long she may have to continue doing so."

"I'm not sure it's a stray if it sleeps in your house, Duncan."

Why did everyone insist on trying to make Tabitha his?

"Aye, 'tis most certainly a stray. I doona own a cat."

She chuckled softly next to him, and he noticed for the first time how lovely her voice really was. Strange to be sure, but lovely.

"If you say so. Look, I hope you don't feel like I pushed you into a job here. If you don't want to be away from home that long, I promise you it is fine. Don't feel obligated to stay here."

"I need the work, lass. There is no' a stone wall nor structure in my homeland that I havena built or fixed. I am glad for the work."

"Oh. Good."

They both turned toward the sound of footsteps coming toward them. The Laird of McMillan Castle approached.

"Madeline, just where do ye think ye are going? Do ye no' see how dark 'tis outside? I ken where ye come from, ye lassies do whatever ye please whenever ye please, but I doona care for the idea of ye walking back to the castle alone in the dark after seeing Duncan to the inn. I will see him there. That way I can go ahead and settle arrangements with Isobel. Go inside and have one of the maids heat some water for a bath. Ye look as though ye could use one. I doona ken if I've ever seen ye look quite so ragged."

Duncan's eyes grew wide at the insult. While the lass looked tired to be sure, ragged would not be the word he would use to describe her. Beautiful, wild, mysterious mayhap, but certainly not ragged.

The reflexive knot in his gut that had built at Baodan's words relaxed when Madeline snorted comically in response.

"Well, geez, thank you, Baodan. You really shouldn't flatter me so." She laughed again and continued. "It's been a long day, okay? And sure, a bath sounds wonderful."

She turned and looked at him. "Goodnight, Duncan. I'll see you tomorrow."

On impulse, he leaned down low to whisper in her ear. "I think ye look lovely, lass. Sleep well, Madeline. Thank ye for yer kindness today."

Without another word, the lass whirled and took off toward the castle at a much quicker pace than she'd left it.

No wonder he was still alone. He'd never had much of a way with the lassies.

Madeline

I was still trembling by the time I made it to my bedroom, but this time my shaking hands had nothing to do with watching my stepmother faint. The feel of Duncan's warm breath against the side of my face had quite nearly undone me. It took me until the tub in my room was fully filled and ready for me before I was able to compose myself.

I was too old for this nonsense. Too old to be lusting after a man I didn't know. Too old to be imagining what he looked like underneath his kilt, and just how good it would feel to have his hands rip my dress right off of me.

Shaking my head, I thanked the young woman who'd drawn my bath and moved to undress in front of the mirror. The moment I gazed back at my reflection, I reared back in horror.

No wonder Baodan had been so blunt. I looked as if I'd spent the past week sleeping in the stables. The day had been so strange and busy that I'd completely forgotten that when exposed to moisture—and without the necessary hairspray I relied so heavily upon in my own time—my hair would balloon up to three times its normal height and size.

I looked ridiculous. Not only was my hair almost out past the width of my shoulders, but the bottom of my dress was caked in mud from the hike back from Henry's. And on top of everything, there was a giant piece of food stuck in between my two front teeth.

Mortified, I scrambled out of my dress and all but dove into the tub, putting my head all the way underneath the water.

Perhaps if I held my breath long enough, the lack of oxygen would help me to forget the entire embarrassing ordeal.

Duncan didn't think I looked lovely—there was no way in hell that was true. He was just a kind man showing me pity.

I might as well have been in the skin of my thirteen-year-old daughter. Mortified by a boy. Embarrassed beyond comprehension. There was no coming back from this. No recovery. Nothing I could do to save face.

I was never leaving my bedroom again.

And that was simply the end of it.

CHAPTER 10

Rosie

*O*nce again, Rosie found herself wide awake while the rest of the castle slept, but this time one of her beloved books wasn't the source of her insomnia.

The events of the day ate at her, churning over and over incessantly as she tried to figure out what she could do.

She loved her new grandmother. She understood her desire to protect Baodan and keep him from feeling the loss of his first wife again.

But her grandmother's decision was wrong. She could feel it in her bones.

If Osla wanted to be back in this castle badly enough to haunt Duncan until he brought her here, Rosie knew being locked deep down in the cellar wouldn't do.

Osla had once been the lady of this castle. She deserved to be put in a place of respect—she deserved to be loved. She deserved to be seen and looked at and acknowledged. If Rosie could do nothing else, she could at least do that.

Rosie glanced around her room as the idea took root. There was so much space in her new room, plenty of places to keep a portrait.

Setting her mind to it, Rosie slipped on her shoes, picked up her candle, and left her bedroom in the dead of night.

She would see Osla out of the cellar and into the best room in the whole castle. It was the least the poor woman deserved.

So what if the portrait really was haunted, Rosie thought to herself?

She'd always wanted to see a ghost anyway.

CHAPTER 11

Duncan

For the first time in a week, he slept dreamlessly. When he woke with the sun, all of the anxiety of the past week was lifted. His mother was right. Returned to her home, the lass in the painting no longer haunted him. If that were the only result of his trip, the journey would've been worth it. But now, with a job secured—a good paying one at that—he found himself almost grateful to the lass for haunting him as he slept. Without Osla's haunted portrait, he would've never had reason to travel to McMillan territory.

A restful night's sleep, a day of hard work ahead of him, and— the thought that appealed to him the most—another chance to speak to the strange and intriguing lass, Madeline. For the first time in a long time, Duncan found himself excited for the days ahead of him.

A soft knock on the door to his room preceded a voice he'd grown quite familiar with over dinner the night before—wee Cooper.

Stepping away from the letter that was now ready to send his mother's way, he rose to answer the door.

"Good morning. Are you hungry?"

Confused, Duncan nodded slowly. "Aye, I am lad. Why are ye here at the inn?"

"I work here." The boy smiled and shrugged. "Well, I say work. It's really more like I volunteer here. I don't really need the money, but I do need to keep myself busy—at least that's what everyone at the castle tells me—and I just love Isobel and Gregor, so I help out here when the inn is really full. She sent me up here to see if you were hungry. She said she has food for us downstairs if you want some."

By God, the lad spoke quickly.

"For us, ye say?"

The young boy shrugged again. "Yeah. If it's all right, I thought I would join you again. I'm pretty hungry too."

"O'course. Give me but a moment to seal me letter, and I shall be right down."

With wax already melting, he sealed the message to his mother, and made the short trip downstairs to breakfast. The entire inn smelled heavenly. Fresh baked bread and some sort of seasoned meat had his stomach growling by the time he reached the table.

As expected, the moment he sat down, Cooper began to speak again.

"How did you sleep?"

"Better than I have in ages. It seems returning the portrait did just as me mother hoped. I am no longer haunted by her."

"Huh?"

Duncan's blood suddenly chilled all the way through as his mistake reverberated through him. How could he be so daft? The boy's familiarity had confused him. Cooper hadn't been the child there when he arrived. It had been Madeline's daughter. This child knew nothing of the haunted painting.

"Ach, nothing, lad. Doona fash over it."

Cooper didn't believe him. The expression in the young boy's eyes made that clear.

"It doesn't sound like nothing. What painting? And what haunting? I *really* don't like ghosts."

"Have ye seen one then?"

"What?" The young boy's voice went up an octave. "Of course not, and I really don't want to either. Is there a ghost haunting you?"

"Nae, lad."

"But there was?"

The child was relentless. Mayhap 'twas a blessing he'd ne'er had any of his own. His patience grew thinner by the second.

"I was speaking nonsense, lad. Please. Leave this be and eat yer breakfast."

Cooper hesitated, but Duncan could see that the boy was incapable of doing as he'd asked. It only took a handful of seconds for Cooper to insist once again.

"It didn't sound like nonsense. You said that now that you'd returned it you were no longer haunted. Where did you return it? The castle?"

The child's voice was still pitchy and panicked. He hurried to reassure him.

"Fine, lad. Ye have worn me down. I will tell ye, but ye must promise no' to tell anyone else. Do ye understand?"

"I promise."

"Aye. I returned a portrait to the castle. Aye, 'twas haunting me, but now that the painting is returned to its home, it will no longer haunt anyone."

"So there *isn't* a ghost at the castle?"

Duncan shook his head.

"You promise?"

He gave the boy one simple nod in assurance.

"Good. Can I ask you one other question?"

Duncan laughed and bit into a piece of steaming hot bread.

"Ye shall anyway."

"Can I work with you today? Help you out? I like learning new things and maybe you could teach me how to do what you do."

Duncan sat silently a moment. The lad was a handful. He wasn't sure he could stand a day of the boy chattering away, but the job was a large one. A helping hand would go a long way.

"If yer Ma and Da doona mind it, and ye promise to do as I tell ye, then aye. I canna pay ye though."

"I don't want you to pay me. I just want to learn."

Duncan smiled. He liked the child. Even if the boy talked far too much.

"Perfect. Then I shall welcome yer assistance."

For the briefest of moments, the two ate together silently before Cooper spoke up again.

"Everyone at the castle really likes you."

Duncan smiled. The wee lad really couldn't help himself.

"Well, I am glad for it. I want those employing me to be satisfied with me service."

"Yeah. Someone at the castle *really* seems to like you."

Not keen to take the child's bait, Duncan continued eating his meal.

"Don't you want to know who it is?"

"No' particularly, lad. I doona care for gossip."

Duncan glanced up from his breakfast to see Cooper frowning.

"I don't gossip. I'm just trying to tell you something that I think you'd like to know. I heard Madeline tell Mom that you were the most exciting thing to happen to the castle since she moved here. And I gotta tell you, Duncan. Ms. Madeline doesn't get excited about much."

Duncan detested gossip, but in this instance, the boy was right.

He did enjoy knowing that Madeline liked him. Mayhap he hadn't made a total dolt out of himself the night before. The next time he saw her, he would make certain to test the waters further.

CHAPTER 12

 hree Days Later

Rosie

Rosie couldn't take it another moment. She couldn't be startled awake for another night. This had to end once and for all.

Returning the portrait to the castle hadn't done what Duncan hoped. Rather than putting the poor woman's soul to rest, the painting had simply moved on from haunting Duncan. Now she spent her nights haunting Rosie, and Rosie couldn't bear another moment of it.

Sure, she'd wanted to see a ghost in theory. And while she hadn't seen an *actual* ghost yet, what she had seen was enough to put her curiosity to rest.

For the third night in a row, Rosie found herself awake in the darkest hours of the night. Only this time, she wasn't going to allow Osla to wake her. This time, she would see it happen in real time. Perched on the end of her bed, her blanket wrapped around her shoulders, candles lit around the room so she could keep a close eye on the painting, Rosie waited.

She would see the painting start to rattle. She would see Osla's eyes shift ever so slightly. She had to see it. She needed to witness the act herself to know for certain that her late-night horror story readings hadn't caused her to imagine all of it.

The first night, it was easy to convince herself that it was only her imagination at play. Tell someone a house is haunted and it won't take long for something to happen to convince them it's true —even if it isn't. Her reading had shown her that much. She imagined a painting could work much the same way.

She'd been told the painting was haunted. Now her mind was working overtime to prove to herself that it was. But it wasn't her imagination that caused the painting to fall from its propped position against her wall, and she swore that Osla's eyes shifted just a little that first night after she lifted her back up into place.

The second night was even more obvious. The corner of Osla's mouth was most assuredly turned up at one side after falling and her eyes looked even more changed.

Still, she'd yet to see anything actually happen. Both nights she'd only witnessed the aftermath after being awakened by a clamor. This time she needed to see it.

One hour passed. Then two. By the third, she was almost convinced that perhaps it had been her mind inventing it all. Maybe the frame was bent at the bottom making it unstable and causing it to fall over onto its face? Maybe she hadn't properly studied Osla's face before and only thought that it had changed.

But then, three and a half hours into her stakeout, something in the room began to shift. A chill washed over Rosie as the air grew cold around her. Reaching up a hand, she quickly rubbed at her eyes to push the sleep away as her hand holding the candle began to shake.

Then, ever so slowly, the portrait began to tremble, back and forth, back and forth against the wall. Rosie wanted to scream but couldn't manage to open her mouth enough to do so. Instead, she gripped her blanket more closely around her shoulders and watched.

Osla's eyes suddenly jerked inside the painting, changing directions until it looked as if she were peering right at Rosie. Rosie locked eyes with Osla's pleading gaze before the painting rocked hard once more and fell onto its face.

"That's it. Enough." Rosie said the words aloud as she stood with the blanket still wrapped around her shoulders. Still shaking, Rosie ran from the room, unsure of just who she intended to seek out until she found herself in front of Cooper's bedroom door.

Knowing that Cooper shared his room with his younger siblings, Rosie pushed the door open as quietly as she could, tiptoeing toward the edge of his bed before placing a hand over his mouth as she lowered herself to whisper into his ear.

"Wake up. I need you."

Rosie couldn't see Cooper's expression in the darkness, but his weary voice struggled to answer against her hand before she released him.

"Ro..Rosie?"

"Yeah, it's me. Come here. I need your help."

Without a word, Cooper rose from his bed and followed her out into the hallway. No matter how much he got on her nerves, she had to admit that Cooper never did let her down when she really needed him.

As soon as Cooper closed the door behind him, Rosie reached for his hand and began to pull him back toward her own bedroom.

"Cooper, I did something I shouldn't have, and I need your help to get rid of it."

Cooper's voice was hesitant as he answered her.

"What did you do?"

"I think it's better if I show you. It's in my bedroom."

Cooper

*H*e couldn't let Rosie see how frightened he truly was. She already thought he was too young—too little—as she so often liked to point out to him. No. Rosie was frightened. That meant he had to be strong for her. This wasn't a ghost. This was just a painting—a haunted painting.

It didn't matter how fast his heart beat in his chest. It didn't matter how tired he was. His Rosie was scared, and he simply had to find a way to be strong for her.

"Why did you take it out of the cellar, Rosie?"

Rosie sighed and shrugged. "I don't know. I felt bad for her. This was her home. I didn't think she needed to be locked away in the cellar as if she didn't belong here. I understand why grandmother didn't want to make Baodan sad, but I just thought she needed to be somewhere where she could be seen."

Rosie was the best girl in the world. Of course she cared about the woman in the painting. It was one of the many reasons that Cooper loved her so much.

"Well, what do you think we should do now?"

Rosie hesitated and a familiar apprehension built in Cooper's gut. Whatever Rosie was about to suggest, he was likely to get in trouble for it. He could sense it in every part of his being.

"I think we should burn it."

"Burn it?" Cooper knew his voice rose too loudly at the question, but it was the last thing he expected her to say.

Consult a grown-up? Likely.

Return it to the cellar? Possible.

Burn it? Never.

"Why would you want to burn it?"

"Maybe she's trapped in the painting, Cooper, and burning it will set her free? Sort of like cremating a body—ashes to ashes and all that."

Cooper shivered at the thought. He didn't want to think about burning the painting—let alone burning bodies.

"Where would we even burn something?"

"Somewhere outside of the village. Far enough away that no one will see the smoke."

Cooper sighed. Just like with the cake—Rosie's mind was set. No matter what he said to her, there would be no talking her out of it.

"I really don't think this is a good idea."

Rosie shrugged. "I don't care. I'm doing it. You don't have to come, if you don't want to."

Rosie knew he would come. She wouldn't have woken him up, otherwise.

CHAPTER 13

Madeline

J saw little of Duncan after his first night here. I would pass him while on my way to Henry's, but he was always so busy working and visiting with his new assistant, Cooper, that we'd only exchanged a polite wave and a smile.

Perhaps it was for the best. While a bout of uncharacteristic optimism had seized me at first, I could now see that pursuing a relationship with anyone in this century was asking for trouble. The men that lived among the modern women at McMillan Castle were not the norm. It wasn't possible for that many more of them in all of Scotland to be so accepting as the group I was acquainted with.

"Ye seem distracted, lass. What's on yer mind?"

I continued to fold Henry's extra linens and did my best to pretend he hadn't just caught me tuning him out.

"Nothing. Nothing at all."

A knock on the door saved me from his further questioning. I quickly set down the pile of laundry and moved to answer it. The delightful innkeeper, Isobel, stood on the other side.

"Good morning to ye, lass. I hoped ye would still be here."

Like everyone else in the village, I adored Isobel. She was one of the most singularly likable people I'd ever met in my life.

"Good morning. It's so nice to see you. Do you need my help with something?"

"Aye. If ye doona mind, I thought ye could drop this basket of food off for Duncan on yer way back to the castle. The silly lad refuses to enter the castle while working, and he willna stop and come back here for food. By the time he arrives at the inn at nightfall, he is ready to eat me out of house and home. I doona mind walking it to him meself if ye shall be a while. I only thought I would see if ye would be headed back that direction soon."

I'd been basically finished with my daily tasks for Henry for well over an hour. I'd simply been stalling to allow him time to have his fill of conversation.

"I'll be heading back that way in just a few minutes. I'm happy to bring it."

"Thank ye, lass. I'll set this just inside."

Stepping around me, Isobel directed her attention to Henry.

"Henry, I havena seen ye in far too long. Are ye well?"

After placing the basket next to the pile of linens I was nearly done folding, I watched as Isobel made her way over to Henry and reached to give his hand a hearty squeeze.

"I am better for seeing ye, lass. Ye and Gregor are well past due for a visit. The two of ye should come for dinner sometime soon."

"We would be happy to. I'll talk to Gregor about it as soon as I get back to the inn."

They visited for a few minutes more, and by the time I was finished folding, Isobel was ready to leave as well. I walked her back to the inn as it was along the path back to the castle.

Isobel said little on the short walk back, but just as we neared the door of her home spoke up beside me. "Ye do ken that Duncan is quite taken with ye, aye?"

Heat rushed to my face. "I know no such thing. He doesn't know me."

Isobel chuckled softly and pointed to my reddened cheeks. "And ye doona ken him either, but that hasna stopped yer cheeks from flushing in excitement at the thought. He asks Cooper about ye all the time."

I glanced down at the basket of food in my hands and then back at Isobel.

"Is this a setup, Isobel?"

She feigned shock. "O'course no', lass. I doona have it in me to be so conniving. Though there is enough food in that wee basket for two should ye find yerself hungry enough to eat by the time ye reach him."

She gave me a wink before disappearing inside the inn.

As if cued by Isobel's words, my stomach growled so loudly that I blushed all over again.

---

*D*uncan's back was toward me as I approached them, and I reveled in the opportunity to watch him interact with Cooper. As usual, Cooper was yammering on about something at a million miles a minute, but Duncan was patient as he continued to guide Cooper through how to set the stones in the section they worked on. I couldn't help but think it a shame that Duncan had no children. I could tell by the way Cooper had taken to him that he would've made a good father.

Cooper spotted me first. Taking note of the large hunk of bread extending past the edge of the basket, he leapt up from his crouched position and bounded toward me.

"Lunch!"

So much for the picnic for two Isobel had tried to arrange.

I smiled at him and reluctantly allowed him to take the basket. "Yes, courtesy of Isobel. She knew I would be headed back to the castle soon and thought you two would be hungry."

"Aye, we are. Thank ye, lass."

Duncan faced me and smiled, and I found myself thankful that once red, my skin tended to stay that way for a while. It meant that it was unlikely he was able to see just how hot I'd suddenly become.

Nervous and fidgety, I started to panic.

"All right. Well, there you go then. I hope you both enjoy it. Looks like the work is coming along well. See you two later."

I spun away from them, but was stopped by a sudden hand on my arm.

"Wait, lass. Do ye mind if I speak to ye a moment?"

I nodded with my back still toward him as he walked around to face me.

As I looked up at him, I noticed that his face was as flushed as mine was, and something inside of me relaxed just a little.

"I hope that ye doona mind, but I've inquired about ye to Isobel while staying at the inn. She has told me that ye've no suitors at present. I…"

He hesitated and I worried that in the silence he might actually be able to hear my heart pounding against my rib cage. Suitor? I wasn't sure I'd ever had a *suitor* in my entire life—just a lifelong best friend who in the end became my husband.

Duncan continued to search for his words as I tried to keep my breathing in check.

"I…the truth is, that I am rotten at all of this, lass. I only mean to say that I think ye are bonny. Would ye join me for dinner at the inn tonight?"

I smiled at him. His nervousness made my own more bearable. "Yes. I would love that."

The expression of surprise that moved over his face at my answer almost caused me to laugh, but I swallowed hard before allowing the noise to escape.

"Really, lass?"

I nodded. "Yes. I wouldn't tease you. Are you sure you want me to?"

He nodded and reached for my hand before lifting it up to his lips as he brushed them against my knuckles. "Aye, lass. Verra sure."

"Good. I'll see you tonight."

It was all I could do to make it inside my bedroom before I leaned against the door and squealed in delight.

I was excited about this. Truly excited about something for the first time in ages.

Maybe I hadn't died along with my husband. Maybe the loss of him had just sent me into hibernation, and my metaphorical spring had finally come.

CHAPTER 14

Cooper

ooper couldn't sleep. His conscience tormented him as he lay awake and stared up at the ceiling in his bedroom. Burning the painting wasn't like sneaking cake before a birthday celebration. This was different. Eating the cake was harmless. This didn't feel so.

Eventually they would be caught. He just knew it.

It wasn't only the dread of inevitably being caught that bothered him. It was that ever since they'd burned it things felt worse in the castle—*more* haunted in some way he hadn't been able to put his finger on just yet.

He'd seen nothing, but he could sense something in the air he was sure wasn't there before.

Rosie had said nothing to him, but he had a feeling that she could sense it too. That maybe their desire to end Osla's haunting hadn't worked as they'd hoped it would.

Cooper sighed and rolled over on his side, pulling his blankets high up above his shoulders. He wanted to get up, to light a candle as he often did while others were sleeping and run downstairs to read or play on his own, but tonight his fear stopped him. Something was off inside the castle, and he didn't want to be alone when he discovered just what that was.

"*I*s something the matter with ye, lad? Ye look as if ye might fall over right where ye stand?"

Cooper jumped at the sound of Duncan's voice behind him. He was meant to be loading up a pile of stones to move further down the fence line, but after a night of no sleep, his arms and legs were weak, and his mind continued to drift no matter how hard he tried to stay on task.

He opened his mouth to answer, but instead a yawn escaped. "I...I'm sorry, Duncan. I didn't sleep at all last night."

Duncan gave his shoulder a firm pat before pointing back toward the castle. "Go inside and have a wee rest. I'll be fine by meself for the rest of the day. Ye've been a big help to me, but I doona think ye shall be so today no matter how hard ye try."

The thought of lying down for a while did sound rather nice to him.

"You sure? You don't mind?"

"O'course no'. I'm no' paying ye, lad. Ye needn't work with me anytime ye doona wish to. I appreciate ye whene'er ye are here, but I doona expect ye to be. Go and enjoy yer day."

That was all Cooper needed in order to set off in the direction of the castle.

Yawning with just about every third step, Cooper moved through the castle as quietly as he could. If any of the younger children saw him before he was able to sneak away for a nap, they would drag him into playing with them. And today, he just didn't have the patience for it.

To his surprise, he didn't cross paths with anyone in the castle until he rounded the hallway corner leading to his bedroom. His grandmother and Baodan stood visiting just a few doors down from his bedroom.

He waved at them but neither waved back. It was only then that he noticed the look of concern on his grandmother's face. He didn't even think either of them had noticed his presence, they were so engrossed in conversation.

Cooper continued on to his room, opening the door and taking one step inside before he heard the one name that caused his little feet to stop cold.

"Osla."

His heart pounded in his chest. He stepped far enough into his room so they couldn't see him, but stayed close enough to the open doorway so he could listen better.

"Ye havena said her name to me in a verra long time, son. What do ye need to tell me about Osla?"

Cooper thought his grandmother's voice sounded shaky as she spoke. He imagined that if he opened his mouth right now to speak, his would be too. He leaned his ear further toward the hallway to listen for Baodan's answer.

"I saw her."

Cooper's legs began to tremble, but he didn't move a muscle. He had to know what Baodan was going to say next.

"What do ye mean ye saw her?"

"I mean precisely that. Last night, as I made me way around our bedchamber to blow out all of our candles, I glanced into the looking glass, and there she was—standing behind me, staring over me shoulder, her eyes as sad as I'd e'er seen them. Mitsy said she'd ne'er seen my face so pale. I still shake when I think of it."

If it hadn't truly been before, his grandmother's voice was definitely shaky as she answered Baodan now.

"Did...did Mitsy see her?"

"Nae. No' then."

"Mayhap ye were overtired. I ken that Osla must cross yer mind from time to time. Mayhap she was on it last night, even if ye dinna realize it at the time."

"Nae." Baodan's voice was firm in his answer. "Ye doona understand. Mitsy dinna see her last night, but she did see her this morning. She woke before me, and Osla was standing at the foot of our bed. Mitsy screamed so loudly I couldna believe the whole castle dinna wake."

Cooper's mind began to reel.

Was that why he'd been unable to sleep the night before? Had some part of him been able to sense Osla's ghost within the castle?

Whatever it was, Cooper knew one thing for sure.

Burning the painting had only made everything so much worse.

They hadn't given Osla any sort of peace.

All they'd done was let her loose, free to roam around the castle tormenting them.

Tears pooled in Cooper's eyes as he slid to the floor and pulled his knees tight to his chest.

What were they supposed to do now?

CHAPTER 15

Madeline

"Mom. You need to take one real big deep breath. Get a grip. It's going to be fine. It's just dinner. You've already eaten dinner with him once before."

I smiled at Rosie, and closed my eyes as I drew in the deepest breath I could manage, which honestly wasn't deep at all. She kept her grip on my arms as she stared into my eyes.

"You look great. Duncan is nice. Just relax."

This wasn't the way this was supposed to work. Rosie wasn't supposed to be reassuring me. I was supposed to be convincing her that it was okay for me to date.

"Are you sure this doesn't bother you? I know it has to feel weird."

Rosie let go of my arms and took one step away from me before crossing her arms and sighing dramatically.

"Mom. It's only dinner. You're not marrying Duncan. And yes, it's fine. Dad's been gone for years now. It's time for you to enjoy yourself again. I'm ready to have my old mom back."

Those words plucked at the ever-present knot of guilt I suspected all mothers feel from the moment their children leave the womb. While my grief after Tim's death seemed unbearable at the time, I could now see that Rosie's grief had been even worse. She hadn't just lost her father. For quite a long time, she'd lost me, as well. I wasn't sure I would ever stop feeling horrible for all that I'd put her through.

"I'm better than I was, surely?"

Rosie nodded and dropped her arms to come and give me a hug. "Much better. But still not the same."

Was anyone ever the same after losing the person that seemed to make the world spin for them? I wasn't sure 'same' was possible.

"I'm not sure I ever will be that person again, Rosie. Not entirely."

With her face pressed against my chest, I hugged her tightly as she answered me.

"I know. But there's got to be more happiness out there for you than you feel right now."

"Are you happy, Rosie?"

She shrugged in my arms. "I'm thirteen. Nobody is happy at thirteen. At least that's what Grandmother told me the other day."

I laughed and bent to kiss the top of my daughter's beautiful red hair.

"Your grandmother's right. Thirteen sucks."

Sensing that Rosie was now fully over her unusual display of affection for me, I released my grip on her and moved to give myself one more check in the mirror.

At least I looked better tonight than I had on the first night Duncan met me.

Rosie was right. It was going to be fine. Even if it wasn't, even if Duncan ended up being a total loser, it was good to feel nervous again—to feel anything again.

THE CURSE OF MCMILLAN CASTLE

Duncan

"*A*ll is cooked and warm for the two of ye. Gregor and I willna move from our room until after the lass has left, I promise ye. Ye willna ken we are here."

Isobel had gone far beyond her duties as innkeeper for him more than once. But tonight's spread of food and candles astounded Duncan as he looked at all that was laid out before him.

"Isobel...I dinna..." Duncan was beside himself. "I dinna mean for ye to go to so much effort, lass. I expected ye to serve what ye usually do. And I dinna mean for ye to run everyone else away from the inn."

She waved a dismissive hand at him. "Nonsense. I enjoyed every bit of it. And sending the one-night stay travelers away has given Gregor and me a chance to have an evening of rest."

Isobel pointed through the window before turning to run upstairs.

"She's nearly here. Have a lovely evening, lad. Ye deserve it."

Madeline

*D*uncan met me at the door, and the sight of him rattled me so much that for a moment, I thought perhaps someone else staying at the inn had simply stepped outdoors as I entered. But the way his lips turned up at the corners, making him look perpetually friendly, was unmistakable. The feast of a man standing before me was most certainly Duncan.

I'd only ever seen him either soaked to the bone from rain, or covered in dirt from work. But cleaned up, in a fresh kilt, with his hair pinned back at the nape of his neck, he was a splendor to look at.

"You…you look great, Duncan."

He chuckled and stepped back inside the doorway to usher me inside.

"'Tis a surprise to me, as well, lass. I canna remember the last time I was no' covered in dirt."

I smiled at him as I slipped off my coat and offered it to him.

"That's not how I meant it. You always look nice. You just look different tonight, is all."

"Ye look lovely, as well, lass."

I turned away so he wouldn't see me blush as I took in the surroundings of the room.

It had Isobel written all over it.

"Isn't Isobel great?"

"Aye. Consider yerself lucky that I dinna cook any of this. I am wretched at it."

I honestly couldn't remember the last time I'd cooked anything.

"That makes two of us. My work has always kept me so busy that I never really mastered the art of home cooking."

He stepped up close behind me to lean around me and pull out the chair at the small table set for us.

"Caring for the elderly, lass? 'Tis noble work."

"That isn't what I've always done. I used to…" I stopped, realizing in that instant that I couldn't tell Duncan the truth about my work in a hospital. He didn't know about the time travel, and it wasn't my call whether or not I could tell him. "I used to have different work."

He must've sensed my hesitation, and I could see him make the decision not to press me on it as he walked around and sat down at the other side of the table.

"If this is half as delicious as anything else Isobel has cooked for me, we willna be disappointed."

"Oh, I'm certain we won't."

Duncan dug in first, and the soft moan of delight that escaped his lips only confirmed the treat I was in for.

"I guess it is half as delicious then?"

"'Tis at least twice as delicious."

He continued to eat while I began to sample the meal. After a short period of silence as we relished in Isobel's cooking, Duncan spoke again. "What happened to yer first husband, lass?"

The question took me by surprise. It was unusual for anyone to ask me about Tim so pointedly. More often than not, no one mentioned him at all. But rather than the usual lump that rose in my throat at the thought or mention of him, all I could think of was how much it pleased me that Duncan wasn't afraid to ask me about him. It was easier to feel okay when people behaved as if you were.

"We lost him suddenly. There was something wrong with his heart—although we didn't know it. One day he just collapsed and didn't get back up again."

"Ach, I canna imagine how difficult that was for ye and Rosie."

"It was. Still is. We're okay, though."

"Have ye had many suitors since then? I would wager that ye have."

I snorted. Loudly. It was not a good sound.

"I've had exactly zero suitors, Duncan. I haven't really had any interest in that."

He said nothing for a moment. When he did speak again his voice was quieter.

"I see. I appreciate ye joining me. I shall enjoy yer company even so."

I didn't understand his meaning. He seemed deflated, saddened by something I'd said, but he moved on from the topic too quickly for me to inquire as to where I'd taken a misstep.

He asked me about Rosie. He spoke about his own home and told stories from his childhood. I hated that so many of my answers to him were lies. Even so, I enjoyed every minute I spent in his company. We chatted for hours. Long after all of the food was gone.

"I shall walk ye back to the castle, lass. I hope ye ken that I wished to escort ye to here from the castle as well, but Isobel insisted I clean meself up before ye arrived. She said that since 'twas still daylight, ye would be fine on yer own."

Mention of walking back to the castle altered the mood in the room. I wasn't ready to leave him, and I got the impression he wasn't ready for me to leave him either. But as I glanced out the window to see the moon high in the sky, I knew it was time to leave.

"Isobel was right. I was fine walking here by myself. I'll be fine walking back if you don't want to make the trip."

Duncan laughed and shook his head. "Do ye no' remember me first night here? Baodan would ne'er allow it. I willna either. Just give me a moment to get me coat from me bedchamber. I will only be a moment."

Duncan

*D*uncan barely made it to his bedchamber door before he heard the sound of Isobel and Gregor's door open. The sound was quickly followed by the soft sound of Isobel's voice behind him.

"'Tis going well, aye?"

He sighed as he faced her. "Nae, lass. Every moment has been torturous."

Isobel's face crinkled up in confusion.

"Nothing about it sounded torturous to me. What are ye talking about?"

Duncan crossed his arms in mock-horror. Of course Isobel had listened in.

"If ye've been listening, as ye plainly have, ye should ken. She doesna wish to have a suitor. She doesna see this night as I do. All night, I've grown madder for her with each passing moment, and all she's done is try to protect me pride by accepting me invitation here. She doesna care for me, lass."

The back of Isobel's hand smacked him hard against the arm.

"Ye are a daft fool. She said no such thing. She was speaking in the past tense, no' the present. Ask her and see for yerself."

Madeline

*W*hatever had happened to him while retrieving his coat, Duncan's mood was entirely different by the time he returned to my side.

Gone was the chatty, funny man I'd been with all night. Instead, as we made our way back to the castle, he was distracted, fidgety, and I could tell that as I spoke to him, he wasn't really listening. I tried to blow it off, but ten minutes into our walk, I'd had enough.

I stopped and called out to him as he continued to walk ahead of me.

"What happened to you?"

He stopped, only then realizing that he'd traveled on ahead as he spun and faced me.

"I'm sorry. What did ye say, lass?"

"You're acting strangely. Like you're not here with me anymore. Are you okay?"

He sighed, shook his head, and moved his hand to his hair as if he meant to run his hand through it, but stopped when he remembered it was pulled back.

"Nae, lass. I must ask ye a question for I fear I may lose me sanity if I doona do so. But I fear I already ken the answer, and no part of me wishes to hear ye say it."

I couldn't begin to imagine any question that should've made him so nervous.

"Okay…ask it then."

"Do ye care for me, lass?"

I frowned at him, as I tried to think back on anything I'd done or said that might make him think otherwise.

"Yes, Duncan. I do. I wouldn't have come to dinner if I didn't."

He sighed, clearly frustrated.

"But the acceptance of me invitation was intended to spare me feelings, aye? Ye doona care for me as I do ye. Ye doona want a suitor."

Ah. That was it then—the reason behind the disappointment that had washed over his face earlier in the evening.

I smiled and walked toward him as he stood awkwardly in front of me. When I reached him, I placed my hands on his chest. I took no small amount of delight from the way his breath caught in response to my touch.

"Duncan...I'm really not that nice of a person. I've never been good at doing anything to spare anyone's feelings. Clearly, you misunderstood me, so let me make it incredibly clear to you now. I wouldn't have come to dinner if I didn't like you. I wouldn't have spent so much time trying to make my hair look nice if I didn't care for you. And Duncan, while I'm not sure if I want a suitor, I am getting more and more sure by the second that I do want you."

He drew in a raspy breath as he stared down at me in the moonlight. "Aye?"

I nodded. "Aye."

His arms came around me quickly then, lifting me towards him as his lips found mine. He kissed me thoroughly, all of it intensified by the closeness of our bodies before pulling back and smiling at me.

"I told ye before that I was no good at this."

I laughed as he lowered me back down to the ground. "I don't know what you're talking about. I quite enjoyed it."

He took my hand as we resumed our walk back to the castle.

"I doona mean the kiss, lass. 'Tis only, if no' for Isobel, I would've left this night certain ye dinna care for me. Ye would no' have seen me again."

No wonder it had taken him so long to get his coat.

"She spoke to you upstairs, then?"

"Aye."

"Then, I will have to give her my own thanks tomorrow, as well."

Duncan kissed me three more times before we made it to the back entrance of the castle.

When we arrived, I gave him one last kiss and reached for the door handle before he stopped me by placing a hand on the door.

"Can I see ye on the morrow, lass? Mayhap we can meet midday and go for a walk in the sunshine?"

"I would love that."

Beaming from ear to ear, I stepped inside to find Kenna standing just inside the doorway.

Clearly she'd been waiting for me.

The giddiness from the moment drained from me as I looked at her.

She looked like death.

CHAPTER 16

"*K*enna, what is the matter? You...you don't look well."

Kenna nodded as if she knew that and shakily reached for my hand. Her demeanor frightened me, and the staunch contrast of the high of thirty seconds earlier made my sudden concern for her more intense.

"Aye, I doona feel well either. I need ye to come with me. I'm too frightened to go and see for meself."

I tried to keep pace as she tugged me through the many hallways of the castle.

"Where are we going, Kenna? What's going on?"

Kenna stopped suddenly, whirling toward me as she pulled me to the side of the hallway and leaned in close, her voice a frightened whisper.

"Baodan came to me today. He saw Osla last night. And Mitsy saw her this morning."

"What?" I frowned at her. "What do you mean, he saw her?"

"'Tis what I asked him. They saw her ghost. Both of them swear it."

I hardly knew what to say. I'd never been much of one to believe in ghosts, but then again, a few years ago I wouldn't have been one to believe in time travel either.

"Well...that's...not great."

It was a stupid response, but it was all that came to mind. Truth was, I'd thought little of the painting since that night. Duncan had seemed so certain that returning Osla to the castle would resolve things that I'd not questioned his logic.

"Nae, lass. It is no'."

"So, where are we going? What do you want to do about it?"

"I am taking ye to the cellar where I left Osla's painting. I need to see if 'tis still there, and I was too frightened to go alone. Since no one else save Rosie kens about what happened that night, it must be ye that comes with me."

She spun away from me and continued her fast clip toward the basement. She reached for a candle off the wall sconce as she pushed open the old wooden door and began the descent into darkness.

"Oh my God."

I stared blankly at the empty spot against the wall.

The painting was gone.

Rosie

"Cooper, we've been sitting here in the dark for hours. I really don't think we're going to see anything. Maybe you just misheard Baodan. We didn't turn her into a ghost. Can we please just go to bed now?"

"No, Rosie. We aren't going anywhere. And I know we didn't turn her into a ghost. We just set the ghost that was in the painting free."

Cooper's voice was firm, frustrated. He rarely sounded that way. It was enough to keep Rosie seated just where she was.

Minutes ticked by. Hours.

Eventually, Rosie couldn't bear it a moment longer.

"I'm done, Cooper. I have to get some sleep. You sit here as long as you want. I'm going to bed."

Grabbing her candle, Rosie pushed herself up from the floor and stomped off into the hallway before falling back against the wall in horror at the sight in front of her.

The moonlight through the window at the end of the long hall cast enough light in front of her to see the silhouette plainly, and after those nights of staring at her in the painting, Rosie would've recognized that face anywhere.

Rosie opened her mouth to scream for Cooper, but no sound came out as Osla's ghost floated toward her.

CHAPTER 17

Madeline

*M*y strong, obstinate daughter was a wreck. Usually, getting into trouble delighted her. Not this time. She knew she'd messed up, and she regretted it to her core. I held her as she cried into my chest.

"It's going to be okay. Baodan is not going to scream at you. We just have to figure out what to do about all of this."

Rosie continued to cry, her voice so muffled I had to strain to understand her.

"No...he...won't. He will never forgive me, and I don't blame him. His dead wife is haunting him thanks to me."

"Listen." I pulled her away from me just enough so that she was looking into my eyes. "Whatever is going on here, you didn't cause it. You two might have changed something by burning the painting, but this all started long ago. We're going to figure it out."

Hours after Kenna and I discovered the painting missing, Cooper and Rosie had burst into my bedroom, both crying hysterically in the wee hours of the night.

I'd been up all night thinking about it—trying to figure out a solution. I'd come to two different conclusions. One, we needed Morna—the meddling witch primarily to blame for all of the time-traveling madness. Two, I needed to be the one to get her—seeing as it was my daughter's bright idea to set Osla's ghost free within the castle.

My midday date with Duncan would have to wait, and I couldn't give him a real explanation as to why.

It broke my heart to think about how my unexplained disappearance from the castle was most assuredly going to come across as if I intended to blow him off, but I couldn't see any other choice.

Kenna, who I also knew had slept little and whom I'd visited with after calming Cooper and Rosie down, had gathered Baodan and Mitsy in the sitting room so we could tell them everything that had happened along with our plan to fix the mess.

Rosie drew in one, long shaky breath, wiped her nose on a handkerchief, and steadied her gaze.

"Okay, Mom. You have my back?"

I smiled and bent to kiss her cheek. "Always, baby."

I allowed her to walk as slowly as she needed to on the way downstairs. I was so focused on making sure she was okay and that she wasn't going to turn around and bolt away from me that it took me a moment to register Duncan's presence in the room when we walked inside.

He looked pale, overwhelmed, and I knew just by looking into his eyes that he knew. His gaze was different as he looked me over —suddenly unsure, as if he no longer had any idea who I was.

"What are you doing here?"

Baodan spoke up from my left. "We waited a long time for ye, lass. Mother has told me what occurred. Seeing as Duncan played a part in all of this, I thought it wise we include him. He kens now, Madeline."

"He knows..." I hesitated, reaching for the answer I already knew.

"The magic, the time travel, all of it, lass."

I didn't take my eyes off of Duncan. I searched his expression for some sort of reaction, but I could read nothing beyond my initial impression of him. He was lost in the state that all of us at McMillan Castle had experienced before—that place where learning the truth upends everything you think you knew about the world. It was understandable if he needed a moment.

"Baodan, I've been thinking about this all night. I'll go straight through right away. Rosie will come with me. I'll try to get to Morna's by nightfall. She will be able to help. I know it."

Baodan gave me a soft smile before turning his attention to Rosie. He stepped forward and pulled her into a gentle hug.

"I am no' angry with ye, lass. I doona blame ye for burning it. 'Twas a logical hope that it would end this."

Baodan's kindness caused Rosie to burst into tears, but this time I knew her tears were different. They were tears of relief, not guilt. Baodan was a good man through and through.

For the first time since Rosie and I entered the room, Duncan spoke. "I'm coming with ye, lass. None of this would've happened had I no' returned the painting."

The thought of taking Duncan to the future with me set alarm bells off in my mind. There was no way that was a good idea.

"I don't think you should."

"I dinna ask for yer permission, lass. I am coming."

"I am too." Cooper's little voice spoke up next to Kenna.

Baodan released Rosie and looked back over at me.

"I've sent all the servants home. Every resident of McMillan Castle will be passing through time tonight. None will return to this time until Osla has finally found true peace. I willna have anyone else terrified by her as we have been."

I immediately thought of Kamden and Harper.

"Well, all right then. I sincerely hope our twenty-first century friends are ready for some company."

CHAPTER 18

While Kamden and Harper were happy to see everyone and eager to accommodate us—with the extra couple in addition to the set of workers who lived permanently at the castle—there simply wasn't room for all of us at the castle in the twenty-first century.

After much discussion, it was decided that Eoghanan, Grace, Cooper, Duncan, Rosie and I would borrow Kamden and Harper's cars and travel into town where we would get a hotel for the night before making the longer journey over to Morna's in the morning. It would free up three rooms in the castle, allowing everyone else to get a good night's sleep.

After changing into the clothes that those of us who were accustomed to time travel had brought with us and seeing Duncan into some of Kamden's clothing, we set off for the hotel.

The car ride with Duncan was something I would forever wish I'd been able to record. Rosie—no longer riddled with guilt, thanks to Baodan's graceful reaction—delighted in watching Duncan grip at the side of his seat every time I wound around a corner or accelerated.

All day he said little, and with Rosie in the car, I was hesitant to discuss much of anything with him.

By the time we arrived at the hotel, the stress of the day finally caught up with Rosie and she was sound asleep by the time I placed the car in park.

"Lass?" Duncan's voice was barely above a whisper as he tried not to wake Rosie.

"Yes."

"Tell me what to do so I doona act a fool as soon as we step inside."

Duncan was handling all of this better than most, but I could certainly understand his apprehension.

I reached out to squeeze his hand. "Don't worry. Grace, and Eoghanan beat us here. She will most likely have our room keys by the time we get inside. Just don't say anything and once we get up to our rooms, I'll come over and show you how to work everything in your room."

He nodded with a nervous gaze as I watched him look past me and up at the small chain hotel. While our brief time at McMillan had allowed him to see some of the small modern-day miracles, such as electricity, I sensed he knew that even more mind-blowing revelations awaited him inside.

Smiling at him, I moved my hand from his and reached behind me to wake Rosie but stopped as Duncan grabbed my arm.

"Doona wake her, lass. I can carry her."

"She's thirteen, Duncan. She's pretty tall too. You really don't have to."

He shook his head and looked down as he tried to unbuckle his seat belt. "I ken how old she is, lass. But she doesna weigh a thing, and she looks as if she hasna slept in days. I doona mind."

Finding the latch to free himself, Duncan opened the car door as quietly as he could before walking around to Rosie's side of the car.

Tears sprang up in my eyes as I watched Duncan tenderly lift my daughter from the car. How many times had my own father carried me to bed as a child after I fell asleep on the couch with a book spread across my chest? And how many times had I awakened the moment he lifted me up, only to quickly feign that I was still asleep so I could enjoy the feeling of being cared for in such a way? More times than I could remember. Rosie had missed out on so much of that.

"Are ye well, lass?" Duncan whispered the question as I stepped out of the car and brushed a rogue tear from my cheek.

"I'm perfect. Let's go."

It was a miracle Duncan didn't drop Rosie as the elevator lifted us into the air. His eyes doubled in size and he muttered something in Gaelic I knew had to be a curse word as he plastered his back against the back wall of the elevator in surprise.

The key card was equally impressive to him. But somehow, despite the flood of new experiences, between entering the rotating doors of the hotel and finally reaching Rosie's bed, he managed to keep a grip on my still-snoring teenager.

When he finally placed Rosie down on the bed, his back audibly cracked as he straightened himself upright. He laughed as he faced me.

"The lass is heavier than she looks."

"I tried to warn you. Thank you, though."

I turned away from him as I slipped my own room key into my back pocket and held onto his in my right hand before waving him out into the hall.

"You ready for a tutorial on your room?"

He nodded, and together we walked two doors down the hallway to Duncan's room.

"Might I try that wee wand this time, lass?"

Tickled by the fact that he'd called the key card a wand—to be fair though, it was a reasonable comparison—I smiled as I faced him and extended the piece of plastic in his direction.

"By all means. Just hover it over the handle until that little light above it turns green."

He smiled as it lit up, beeped and opened as he turned the handle.

"Must we go back after we retrieve this witch ye speak of?"

Laughing, I pointed to the slot above the lights and gestured so he would know to place the key inside so the lights would turn on.

"So you like this time, then? You're not completely terrified?"

As the door shut behind me and Duncan stepped close to place the keycard where I'd directed him, he surprised me by ducking his head and kissing my cheek.

I immediately warmed all over.

"Nae, I am no' terrified. 'Tis a relief to ken why ye lied to me. I knew ye were no' from London, and aye, what's no' to like? Seems time has brought a fair number of things into being that make life easier. Why would ye e'er choose to live in the past as ye do when ye doona have to?"

I shrugged and followed him as he stepped further into the room.

"My dad was in the past. He's really the only family Rosie and I have left. And we needed a fresh start."

He gave me an understanding nod and then shifted awkwardly from one foot to the other.

"You all right?"

He shook his head. "Nae, lass. I doona wish to embarrass ye, but I need to relieve meself rather urgently. I see no chamber pot."

I laughed and waved him into the bathroom where he immediately looked skeptically down at the toilet.

"In there, lass?"

"Yes." I wasn't sure how to delicately address all of the ins and outs of a toilet to Duncan, but I knew it wouldn't help him at all if I danced around the subject. "Okay, forgive my bluntness, but I'm just going to lay it out for you."

He gave a soft chuckle and a nod before crossing his arms and staring down into the toilet with earnest.

As quickly as I could manage, I explained when to lift and lower the seat, what toilet paper was for, and how to get rid of everything when he was finished. When I stopped, he immediately reached for the buckle on the jeans Kamden had leant him. I hurried from the room as he called after me.

"Thank ye, lass. I believe I can manage it."

Closing the door between us, I moved into the center of the room, unsure of what to do. Should I leave now that he was safely in his room? Should I stay in case he had any other questions? If he got his hands on the television remote, he would definitely have more than a few.

Should I stay for any other reason? For the first time since meeting him, Duncan and I were truly, really alone. What would it be like to be with him? To have his hands roam over me, to feel someone inside me for the first time in years?

My nipples hardened at the thought and I took two steps away from the bed so I would be less tempted to undress and hurl myself into it.

Just as my mind began to drift to even dirtier thoughts, I heard the sound of the toilet flushing as Duncan let out a hearty scream.

I laughed, and hurried to the bathroom door.

"I'm sorry. I should've warned you it would be loud when you flushed it."

He groaned again and I thought I heard something hit the wall in the bathroom.

"Nae, lass. 'Tis no' that. I've..." he hesitated. "I've injured meself on these damn bindings."

Bindings? It took me a moment to think through what he could mean, but as he groaned once more, the answer came to me.

His pants. For a Scot who'd never worn anything other than a kilt or cloth breeches his entire life, Kamden's jeans had to be restrictive for him.

I hadn't the slightest clue what to do.

"Uh. Was it the zipper?"

His voice was tight and pained as he answered me.

"I doona have the damnedest idea what a zipper is, lass. All I ken is that me bollocks have been caught in the teeth of this wretched garment."

Don't laugh. Don't laugh. Don't laugh. I repeated the mantra in my mind as I gritted my teeth and pondered over what to do.

"Duncan. Okay. Don't pull up anymore. You're...you're going to have to pull down to release it. It's going to hurt."

He groaned again and banged his fist against the wall. I hoped the rooms were soundproof. Otherwise, Grace, Eoghanan, and Cooper must be wondering what in the world was going on.

"Are you okay? Do you need me to come in there and help?"

"Nae, lass. I have freed meself, though I willna be putting on this damned garment again this night."

Without another word, he flung open the door to the bathroom and stood before me stark naked from the waist down save for the hand he kept over his crotch to cover his penis. I jumped at the shock of suddenly seeing him bare.

"Oh. I'm sorry. Do you want me to turn away while you get in bed?"

He frowned at me. "Why would ye do that, lass? I doona care if ye see me arse. Ye can see behind me hand as well if ye wish it. I just dinna wish to offend ye."

He still hurt. As he stepped toward me and turned to walk toward the bed, he hobbled awkwardly with each step.

His "arse" was incredible. It reminded me of Brad Pitt's backside in the opening scene of *Troy*. Perfectly firm, muscular, and so cuppable that I wanted to reach out and squeeze it.

He moaned again as he pushed away the top pillows and lifted the covers to crawl inside.

"I am sorry, lass. Pinching one's bollucks will put ye in a foul mood."

I laughed and reached for the door handle to his room. "That's totally understandable. I'll just give you a quick rundown of the rest of the room and leave you for the night."

I slowly made my way around the room, stopping at each lamp and light to show him how it worked. When that was done, I reached for the television remote and moved to sit on the other side of his bed next to him.

"If you can't sleep, I imagine you might spend some time playing with this contraption. Ready to have your mind blown?"

"Blown, lass?"

Laughing, I clicked on television. "Blown is a good thing."

His eyes mimicked what they'd done in the elevator as the screen lit up and noise began to come through the speakers.

"What in the name of Brighid is this, lass?"

"It's a television. You can watch recorded stories or news."

Duncan frowned and reached up to cover his ears. "I doona care for it. Might ye turn it off?"

Surprised, I did as he asked. "Of course. You sleepy?"

He shook his head and reached for my hand. "Nae. No' at all. Do ye think Rosie shall wake again in the night?"

My chest tightened and fluttered again as hope that he might ask me to stay began to rise.

"I doubt it. She's a sound sleeper, and like you said earlier, she looked as if she needed it. Why?"

Duncan shrugged shyly as he squeezed my hand. "I doona wish to offend ye, lass. I doona ken if I should ask what I wish to."

"Please do ask it. I promise you I'm not easily offended."

"Stay with me, lass. Let me hold ye. Kiss ye. Learn more about ye. We needn't do anything ye doona wish to."

I kicked off my shoes and leaned down to kiss him.

"I want to do everything, Duncan. Opportunities like this— privacy, a good bed, a hot shower, someone like you to spend time with—I want to take advantage of it. I'm not sure you're up for *all* of it though."

I cast a quick glance down to where his injured bits were underneath the covers.

He laughed and pulled me toward him.

"I've a feeling a few more kisses from ye shall heal me. At the verra least, let us find out, aye?"

CHAPTER 19

Duncan

Could one die of pleasure? His night with Madeline made him wonder. Even his injured privates hadn't been enough to deter how desperately he wanted her. It was a need unlike anything he'd ever experienced. Over and over they came together during the night, each time more intimate, more loving than the time before.

It wasn't only the meeting of their bodies. The conversation and their shared laughter throughout the night had filled up some lonely well inside of him he didn't even know existed. He could say things to her he'd never told anyone before, and he couldn't help but feel that she was just as comfortable around him.

It was unlike him to move so quickly—to take so much—to move so boldly with anyone. But Madeline wasn't like anyone else. The lass knew her own mind. If she wanted him, he wasn't going to try to convince her otherwise.

Madeline slept soundly against his chest as morning broke, but sleep couldn't seem to catch him as his mind raced.

He now knew one thing for sure.

He had no plans to leave McMillan territory. He would see every stone structure for miles set right if he needed to. His home was no longer the place he'd left behind. His home was wherever this strange, bonny lass existed.

He couldn't tell her this. Not yet. Not so soon.

Not while they all still had the matter of Osla's ghost to attend to.

But once all was settled, he would. And to hear her return his feelings would be the grandest day of his life.

She felt as he did, he knew.

Not one part of him doubted it.

CHAPTER 20

Madeline

*D*uncan had to wake me at sunrise. After being sweetly pulled from sleep by kisses trailed down my neck, I panicked the second I took in the surroundings of the hotel room as my sex-doused brain remembered Rosie in the hotel room two doors down.

Dressing more quickly than I thought possible, I yanked on my pants, reached for my shirt which now lay crumpled up on the floor, bent to give Duncan a quick kiss on the cheek, and fled his room in my rush to try to save face with my daughter.

I relaxed the moment I pushed open the door, and the sound of her soft snoring reached my ears.

The panic returned, however, as I stepped further into the room and the sound of her snore turned into soft laughter.

As I flipped on one of the bedside lamps, Rosie slowly sat up in the bed.

"I knew if I pretended I was still asleep, you'd think you'd gotten away with it."

My cheeks flooded with heat as I tried to think of something that could explain away the situation.

"I don't know what you're talking about. I just got up to see if there was any coffee downstairs in the lobby. I've been here all night."

Rosie snorted and rolled her eyes at me. "Mom, I woke up at one in the morning and watched television for three hours. You weren't here at all last night. It's fine. Just don't say anything else about it. I promise I'll throw up if you do."

She pretended to gag then walked to the bathroom without another word. I heard the shower turn on and, humiliated, I shrunk beneath the covers.

No teenager needed to be aware of their mother spending the night with anyone. She played it cool, but she had to be mortified.

I was officially the worst mom ever.

I said nothing to Duncan on the long car ride to Morna's later that morning. I was now so cognizant of Rosie's presence that I worried about anything either of us might say making her uncomfortable.

I still didn't know where things would lead with Duncan, and until I did, I wanted Rosie's investment in our relationship to be as limited as possible. While my night with Duncan had been amazing, we'd spoken little about the future, and I couldn't help but feel like that was likely because he wasn't planning one.

Why would he be? We barely knew one another, and McMillan territory was not his home. He had responsibilities that would be difficult to manage from this distance. His elderly mother needed him. And whether Duncan wished to admit it or not, I was pretty certain he was the owner of a cat that would surely be missing his care.

Not only that, but each day I watched Duncan and Cooper's progress on the stone work with interest, and I knew they had little left before the job was done. When the work was finished, he would leave, and any interest he believed he had in me would vanish with his desire to return home.

And that, I supposed, was as it should be. Our short time together was something we'd both needed. I needed to be reminded that I could truly feel something other than numbness and anger at my own life, and Duncan needed to learn that those things that had evaded him in life so far—companionship, a wife, and a family—could be his if he ever decided he truly wished it, even if he didn't find those things with me.

I wasn't a child. I could understand that some things are only meant to come into our lives for a season. Perhaps, Duncan was only meant to be just that, a brief respite from my daily routine to remind me that some parts of me hadn't been buried with my husband.

While it wasn't what I wanted, I could make peace with that.

I would have to if my suspicions about him were right.

I sighed as I made the last turn onto the gravel road leading to Morna's inn, and Duncan reached over to squeeze my hand that rested on the gear shift in response. The gesture was an acknowledgment of the realization I suspected we both knew.

Last night was amazing, but it was likely all we were ever going to get.

CHAPTER 21

Cooper

C ooper's body all but vibrated with excitement as Jerry pulled the car out of park and began to drive away from the inn. With Morna riding in the passenger seat and his mother allowing him to ride with Morna and Jerry back to the castle, all was right in Cooper's world once again. He loved it when Morna and Jerry traveled into the past—even if they were only doing so to fix his and Rosie's mistake.

Even Rosie had been allowed to ride with them. All of his favorite people were in one place for the first time in ages.

In all honesty, he couldn't even bring himself to feel bad for what he and Rosie had done. While he regretted that Osla's ghost had frightened everyone—himself included—the fact that their actions had forced them to involve Morna meant that the woman's soul might finally find some rest after the spell was cast.

How could anyone possibly feel bad about that?

"Morna?"

Cooper smiled at her as she turned in her seat to look at him.

"Aye, lad?"

"Why don't you and Jerry just move to the past with us? I miss you every day that I don't get to see you. Things would just be so much better if you were there."

Morna closed her eyes as she reached back to squeeze his knee. When she opened them, Cooper thought he could see tears in her eyes.

"Ach, lad. Ye canna ken how much it means to me that ye love us so, but me place isna where yers is. It hasna been for a verra long time. There is still much work I must do here."

Rosie spoke up beside him. "What exactly is your job, Morna?"

"'Tis no' a job, truly. 'Tis more me passion. I am quite fond of making love matches across time."

Cooper smiled as Rosie glanced over at him with dubious eyes. "Why across time?"

Morna shrugged. "Some of us are born out of time, lass, and 'tis me gift to fix that."

Cooper watched as Rosie contemplated.

"So did you have something to do with the painting? Are you trying to set up Duncan and my mom?"

Morna hesitated for a brief moment before replying. "I'll answer ye honestly, though I fear ye may think less of me for it. I did no' bind Osla's soul to that painting. 'Tis much darker magic than I've e'er had a mind to do. While I doona suppose any of us shall e'er ken for certain, I believe Osla bound herself to the painting when she ken someone within the castle meant her harm, not understanding what the curse would mean for herself after her death.

"That being said, I did come to ken of the painting some time before ye all came to ask for me help. And I may have made some effort to insure the painting found its way to Duncan, sure that he would be led to do the right thing and return it to McMillan

Castle, and that ye and yer mother would be at the castle when he did so."

Cooper could see that Rosie was thinking over Morna's words, so he spoke up in her stead.

"So they are supposed to be together then? Duncan and Ms. Madeline?"

Morna nodded. "I believe they would make a fine match. But I will do nae more than I have to secure it. They are well on their way to seeing that for themselves. The rest is up to them."

Cooper laughed. "That's not like you."

"What can I say, lad? Mayhap I am becoming less forceful in me old age."

"Morna, why did you say we would think less of you? I don't see what you did wrong."

Morna sighed, and returned her gaze to the road in front of them. "'Tis only that I kenned of the lassie's trapped soul and did nothing until ye came seeking me help. 'Tis no' kind. Though in the realm of souls, a few moons is nothing. The lass has been trapped there for years. I dinna think a few more weeks would do her harm if it meant two others found love in the meantime. Still, 'tis morally questionable behavior."

Cooper was no longer listening to Morna's explanation. He knew that Morna always had a good reason for whatever she chose to do. Instead, his attention was back on Rosie, who seemed lost in thought.

He reached out and tapped on her leg. "Are you okay?"

Rosie blinked as if pulling herself from her thoughts and turned to smile at him. "Yeah, I'm okay. Just thinking."

Cooper said nothing, but anxiety built in him. Lately, it never seemed to fair well for him when Rosie got to thinking too much.

Rosie

Rosie knew her judgment of Duncan had been right. Straight away, she'd liked him. Now she knew why. Only problem was, Rosie knew her mother well. If there was any way for her to mess things up, she would.

Rosie didn't understand it—her mother's addiction to unhappiness. Rosie thought about her father every single day, but she knew that he wanted her to be happy. He would have wanted the same for her mother, too. Rosie knew it as surely as she'd ever known anything.

Duncan's stonework at McMillan Castle was almost complete. As quickly as Duncan and Cooper progressed, Rosie didn't imagine they had more than a handful of days left. She would have to be on high alert, for any sign that her mother was attempting to sabotage her relationship with Duncan.

Her mom needed this. And she needed her mom to be truly happy once again.

Rosie looked over at Cooper, knowing she owed an apology to the sweet boy who always did so much more for her than she ever did for him.

"Hey, Cooper."

"Yeah?"

"I'm sorry that I've dragged you into stuff you didn't really want to do lately. I want you to know that you really are pretty much my best friend at this point. I know I'm not as kind to you as I should be most of the time."

Cooper smiled big before giving her a wink and waving a dismissive hand. "It's okay, Rosie. Things have been weird lately. I know you're my friend. I'll always have your back, no matter what."

Rosie grinned at him, hoping that those words were true and he would help her one more time. "So, you're in on my next plan?"

Cooper sighed and crossed his arms. "Can we at least wait another month before getting in trouble again?"

Rosie laughed and shook her head. "We can definitely wait another month to get into any more trouble, but we aren't going to get into any with this plan." Rosie paused and leaned in close to whisper. "We're only going to step in to make sure that all of what Morna has already done doesn't go to waste. We're going to do all we can to make sure Mom and Duncan stay together."

Cooper pulled back, smiled, and gave her a thumbs up. "I'm in then. One hundred percent."

CHAPTER 22

Duncan

*H*ours of silence from Madeline tormented him. What could he possibly have done to upset the lass so? The first car ride from the hotel to Morna's had been difficult enough to bear, but at least then, he believed her silence was to keep from speaking in front of Rosie. But now, as the two of them rode alone on the way back to McMillan Castle, he knew Rosie had nothing to do with it.

Each time he opened his mouth to speak, he thought better of it. The stern expression on Madeline's face made it clear she had no desire for conversation.

How could things have turned so quickly?

Mayhap she worried over what might happen once they returned to the castle? If the old witch's spell didn't take, there were few options left to them.

That must be it, surely. Nothing else had occurred that should've soured her mood so completely.

Bracing himself, he reached up to gently caress the back of her head, hoping she would appreciate his attempt to comfort her.

"I truly do believe 'twill be all right, lass. The witch seems confident she can break the curse that binds Osla here. We should be excited for this night. It means the poor lass may finally rest."

Madeline's brows pulled together as she glanced over at him. "Huh?"

"Madeline, ye've said nae more than five words to me since I woke this morn. I thought ye might be worried o'er the spell we intend to cast this eve."

She shook her head once and returned her gaze to the road. "No. Morna's entirely capable. I honestly haven't thought much of it."

Frustration replaced his anxiety and worry for her. Could she not see how hurtful her behavior was?

"Then, do ye wish to tell me what is wrong, lass? Have I done something to anger ye that I'm nae aware of?"

Again, the same curt shake of her head. If not for the unbearable confines of the jeans he found himself bound in and the heavy sweater he wore, Duncan was certain he would've been able to feel frigid air wafting right off of Madeline's skin.

"No. You didn't do anything. I'm fine."

Duncan laughed and shook his head, shifting in his seat so he stared right at her profile.

"I doona claim to be an expert on women, lass. But I do ken enough to ken that when women deny being upset in such a way, they usually are verra upset indeed."

Madeline sighed, and her shoulders relaxed just a little. "I'm not upset, Duncan. You didn't do anything. I'm just sitting here trying to figure out how to tell you what I've decided."

"What ye've decided, lass?"

"Yes. Look, I want you to know how much I enjoyed last night, how much I enjoyed our dinner together the other night. Duncan,

I truly have loved every minute I've spent with you since you arrived at McMillan Castle."

Duncan's chest began to ache. He knew where this would lead. Madeline wouldn't be the first lass to make him hope for more only to devastate him with a few wretched words. But this sudden change of Madeline's heart, hurt worse than all the others before. He'd been so certain she felt as he did.

With every part of him hurting, Duncan inhaled and braced for what he knew was coming. "But ye doona want me, lass?"

"It's more complicated than that, Duncan. You're almost finished with your work at McMillan. You'll leave once you're done."

"Aye, but..."

"Stop. If you're leaving, then there's really no point to any of this. Let's just both be glad for the fun time we had together and part as friends."

"Lass..."

She interrupted him once more. "No, Duncan. Let's please not argue about it. I don't want either of us to be angry. I really do want to be friends when you leave here."

"O'course I am no'..."

Once more, Madeline began to yammer away at him.

He'd stopped listening entirely. As Madeline continued to rattle away, Duncan's confidence returned. The lass hadn't said she didn't want him. Rather, her nervous speech was a sure sign she did.

Instead, Duncan simply cleared his throat, crossed his arms, and waited for Madeline's chattering to cease. When she finally finished, Duncan spoke forcefully.

"Lass, if ye interrupt me again, I swear to ye, I shall take the wheel and drive us into the nearest tree, if only to keep ye from talking."

He watched as Madeline's mouth began to creep open, and he continued before she could derail the conversation once again.

"Nae, lass. Hush yer mouth. I doona ken what has spooked ye, but I've allowed too many good things in me life to pass because I allowed me fears to creep in. I am too old for such nonsense now. And ye are as well, whether ye realize it or no'. Now listen to me, and listen well.

"Aye. I am nearly finished with me work for Baodan, and aye, I shall return home once finished, but only to fetch me wee cat and me mother. I've every intention of making McMillan territory me home. While I've no' yet spoken to Baodan about any of this yet, as I ken his mind is filled with what we must take care of tonight, I intended to speak with him once Osla's ghost is put to rest. Me hope is that rather than pay for me work, he will allow me to rent a parcel of land from him and allow me a few months to build up me work here before charging me rent on the land. I believe he will be agreeable.

"So, as ye see, there is only one real question that remains. I do want ye, lass. I wouldna uproot me life if I dinna, but ye dinna answer the question I asked ye before. Do ye want me or doona ye?"

Duncan thought he could see a tear spring up in the corner of Madeline's eye, but she kept her gaze forward as she answered him. "Dammit, I really wish I wasn't driving right now, and I'm squashed in the middle of Grace and Jerry, so I can't even pull off to the side without them thinking something is the matter."

Madeline paused and inhaled a shaky breath. "Are you sure you really like me enough to move here, Duncan? You barely know me."

Duncan smiled and leaned across the center console in the car to kiss Madeline's cheek before brushing away her tear with his thumb.

"I ken all that I need to, lass. Now, answer me question."

"Yes, Duncan. Of course I want you."

"I am glad of it. For I want ye more than I've e'er wanted anything in me life."

He kissed her cheek once more before leaning back into his seat, his manhood hard as it strained against the confines of his borrowed jeans.

He groaned as he pushed down on himself, willing his need for her away.

"By God, lass. I take back all the bonny things I said last night about this time. Not a one of them is worth it if one must wear this wretchedly painful garment. My cock will ne'er be the same after the past two days."

Madeline laughed so hard the car quickly swerved to the left and she corrected its course before glancing down at his crotch.

"To be fair, you're not really wearing the correct size of jeans. It's just all that Kamden had for you."

He shook his head, unconvinced. "I doona care, lass. Any size would still be torture on one's bollocks."

Madeline continued to laugh at him as McMillan Castle finally came into view.

CHAPTER 23

Madeline

After we all crossed back over into the seventeenth century and settled into the grand hall for Morna to cast her spell, it occurred to me that my own mood stood in stark contrast with the moods of everyone else in the room.

While the rest of McMillan Castle's residents seemed anxious for the spell and what might or might not happen as a result of it, all I could think of was how full my heart felt. For the first time in years, the possible future before me filled me with hope rather than dread.

Still, understanding the seriousness of the situation, I tried my best to hide my smile as I settled down onto a loveseat with Rosie and tucked her in close as we watched Morna begin her work.

For a while, she fiddled around in the room, scattering objects she'd packed with her, until we all sat inside the boundary she'd created. Once she was finished, she turned to address us.

"When I begin, Osla's spirit will be called to this space, so doona let her sudden presence concern or frighten ye. She will be relieved to be called forward this time, I am sure. The curse Osla placed on herself is no' a difficult one to break, and it shouldna take me long to release her into the next place. I only ask that ye all remain as still as ye can be."

Without a word, Rosie reached over and sought the comfort of my hands. I gave them a tight squeeze as Morna began uttering her incantations.

Once Morna began, it didn't take long for Osla's ghost to appear. To my surprise, the translucent figure resembled nothing of the frightening, banshee-like creature I'd imagined after Cooper and Rosie's retelling of their encounter with her. Instead, she appeared peaceful, relieved even, and I couldn't help but believe that some part of her knew that the witch's presence meant her long nightmare had finally come to an end.

Morna continued her recitation, and as Osla's figure began to fade, the ghost quickly scanned the room. I knew she sought Baodan. When she found him, I watched Baodan's breath catch as he locked eyes with his late wife. His eyes filled with tears as Mitsy reached for his hand. Wordlessly, Osla made her way over to Baodan, and slowly she lifted her right hand and placed it upon his cheek.

A lump rose in my own throat as I watched Baodan reach up to place his own hand over Osla's ghostly one. He smiled at her, gave her a gentle nod, and with that, she was gone.

Peace filled the room.

Osla's curse on herself and McMillan Castle was finally lifted.

hree Days Later

Cooper

"We have to hurry, Rosie. Duncan and I finished our work this afternoon, and he said he was leaving for home early tomorrow morning. I bet he's already at the inn. We gotta catch him before he goes to bed."

Cooper watched as Rosie nodded and hurriedly continued to light the candles they'd so carefully scattered around the room.

With the help of the castle cook, Rosie and Cooper had created a romantic feast for Duncan and Madeline to enjoy together—if only they could convince them to go along with their plan.

"I'm hurrying as fast as I can, Cooper. We need to make sure everything is perfect. Do you have the bag of petals?"

Cooper reached for the rose petals they'd gathered from the village and began to delicately scatter them over the table.

"Okay. Let's go. It's almost dark out."

Together, they looked over the room one last time before hurrying from the sitting room. As they rounded the corner leading to the back door of the castle, they stopped short at the sight in front of them.

Madeline and Duncan were wrapped in each other's arms, kissing—right out where anyone could see them.

"Mom...ew!"

Rosie's voice was horrified as Cooper snickered at the sight. At least it wouldn't be hard to get them to enjoy a romantic meal together.

With red cheeks, Cooper watched as Duncan and Madeline peeled themselves away from one another to face them.

Madeline spoke first, her nose crinkled up in an apology.

"Sorry, Rosie. You two are usually sitting down at the dining table right about now. What's going on?"

With Rosie's mouth still agape in horror, Cooper spoke. "We were pretty sure you two were going to mess up your relationship and you'd need somebody to help you see the way. We cooked a romantic dinner for the two of you."

Madeline's brows lifted in surprise. "Oh. Well, that's awfully kind of the two of you, but no, we're doing just fine."

Rosie crossed her arms and furrowed her brows. As Cooper watched the two of them talk, Cooper couldn't help but notice how much Rosie looked like her mother when she frowned.

"But you haven't said a word about Duncan since the night we spent in the hotel. I've been afraid to ask you about him for fear you might cry."

Madeline sighed. "I'm sorry. I just thought it would be easier to talk about it with you while Duncan was away. He's leaving tomorrow to help move his mother here and to bring back his cat. But he's not *leaving*, leaving. He'll be back."

Cooper smiled, pleased that once again Morna's matchmaking had come through in the end.

"So you don't really need a romantic dinner?"

Duncan laughed and spoke up for the first time. "Nae. We've already eaten. Isobel prepared dinner for us at the inn. Why doona the two of ye go and enjoy the labors of your work?"

Food. Flowers. Candles. Rosie. Nothing in the world sounded better to Cooper.

"Sure! Sounds great to me."

Rosie whirled around to face him, her finger pointing directly at him. "You listen to me, Cooper. I'm hungry, so that's the only reason I'm agreeing to this. But it's just a friendly dinner, you got me? There's nothing romantic about it."

Cooper smiled and gave her a nod. "I've got you. Friendly dinner. That's all."

For now, Cooper thought to himself as he followed along behind Rosie to the opulent meal that awaited them.

Only for now.

CHAPTER 24

*S*ix Months Later

Madeline

*D*ays turned into weeks, and weeks into months, and as time went by, my affection for Duncan—and his for me —only grew. While Tim would always be a part of me, I now knew that I was capable of loving as fully and fiercely as I had before.

It didn't take long for Duncan to build himself a flourishing business and a reputation for fine stonework amongst the villagers in McMillan territory, and his new home on his rented land was nearly complete. Although—as settled as he'd become inside the castle—I doubted either of us would spend much time there. Still, it was nice to know we had the option to get away for a while if we wished it.

Tabitha—as I now knew her—was most assuredly Duncan's cat,

and even she seemed to love the space and freedom she had to roam within the castle.

Perhaps, the biggest surprise of all during the months that followed Duncan's move here was his mother's newfound romance with my favorite client, Henry. While we'd initially settled her into a long-term room at Isobel's and Gregor's inn, Isobel had reported to us that as of late, she rarely dined at the inn. Instead, each night she made the short walk over to Henry's where she would cook for the two of them.

Free from the curse, none at McMillan Castle saw Osla again after the night of Morna's spell, and Rosie, Cooper, Baodan and Mitsy were able to sleep soundly once again.

Smiling as I looked over at Duncan still sleeping in my bed, I thought of just how much had changed in me during the past year. While Duncan and I spoke little of where things were heading in our relationship, we both knew where the other stood.

No matter what, we would be at each other's side—loving, cherishing, and challenging one another.

---

*S*ign up for text messages or my newsletter to be notified when the next book in the series, *Love Beyond Magic - Book 13, releases.*

READ ALL THE BOOKS IN MORNA'S LEGACY SERIES

Love Beyond Time (Book 1)

Love Beyond Reason (Book 2)

A Conall Christmas - A Novella (Book 2.5)

Love Beyond Hope (Book 3)

Love Beyond Measure (Book 4)

In Due Time – A Novella (Book 4.5)

Love Beyond Compare (Book 5)

Love Beyond Dreams (Book 6)

Love Beyond Belief (Book 7)

A McMillan Christmas - A Novella (Book 7.5)

Love Beyond Reach (Book 8)

Morna's Magic & Mistletoe - A Novella (Book 8.5)

Love Beyond Words (Book 9)

Love Beyond Wanting (Book 10)

The Haunting of Castle Dune - A Novella (Book 10.5)

Love Beyond Destiny (Book 11)

Love Beyond Boundaries (Book 12)

The Curse of McMillan Castle - A Novella (Book 12.5)

And More to Come...

SWEET/CLEAN VERSIONS OF MORNA'S LEGACY SERIES

If you enjoy sweet/clean romances where the love scenes are left behind closed doors or if you know someone else who does, check out the new sweet/clean versions of Morna's Legacy books in the Magical Matchmaker's Legacy.

Morna's Spell
Sweet/Clean Version of *Love Beyond Time*

Morna's Secret
Sweet/Clean Version of *Love Beyond Reason*

The Conall's Magical Yuletide
Sweet/Clean Version of *A Conall Christmas*

Morna's Accomplice
Sweet/Clean Version of *Love Beyond Measure*

Jeffrey's Only Wish
Sweet/Clean Version of *In Due Time*

Morna's Rogue
Sweet/Clean Version of *Love Beyond Compare*

Morna's Ghost
Sweet/Clean Version of *Love Beyond Dreams*

Morna's Vow
Sweet/Clean Version of *Love Beyond Belief*

SUBSCRIBE TO BETHANY'S MAILING LIST

When you sign up for my mailing list, you will be the first to know about new releases, upcoming events, and contests. You will also get sneak peeks into books and have opportunities to participate in special reader groups and occasionally get codes for free books.

Just go to my website (www.bethanyclaire.com) and click the Mailing List link in the header. I can't wait to connect with you there.

ABOUT THE AUTHOR

BETHANY CLAIRE is a USA Today bestselling author of swoon-worthy, Scottish romance and time travel novels. Bethany loves to immerse her readers in worlds filled with lush landscapes, hunky Scots, lots of magic, and happy endings.

She has two ornery fur-babies, plays the piano every day, and loves Disney and yoga pants more than any twenty-something really should. She is most creative after a good night's sleep and the perfect cup of tea. When not writing, Bethany travels as much as she possibly can, and she never leaves home without a good book to keep her company.

If you want to read more about Bethany or if you're curious about when her next book will come out, please visit her website at: www.bethanyclaire.com, where you can sign up to receive email notifications about new releases.

Connect with Bethany on social media or visit her website for lots of book extras:

www.bethanyclaire.com

ACKNOWLEDGMENTS

To Rori Bumgarner, Karen Corboy, Elizabeth Halliday, Johnetta Ivey, Vivian Nwankpah, and Pamela Oviatt—thank you so much for your continued work on this series. You all have no idea just how much your eyes help, and I appreciate your time and your input more than you know.

Mom—thank you for your willingness to read these stories. You make the books better, and I'm so glad you're a part of them.

CPSIA information can be obtained
at www.ICGtesting.com
Printed in the USA
LVHW091934141220
674158LV00015B/235/J